Forbidden HEIR

USA TODAY BESTSELLING AUTHOR
MICHELLE HEARD

Cover Designer: Sybil Wilson, PopKitty Design

Cover Model: Pat Tanski

Photographer Credit: Wander Book Club Photography

TABLE OF CONTENTS

Dedication

18 Books.
3 years and 6 months.
Here we are, saying our last farewell to the worlds
of Indie Ink & CRC Holdings.

What started as a five-book series
became so much more.
Della meeting the screw crew... that moment
changed more than just her life.

Thank you for loving these characters
as much as I do.
I hope they gave you as much joy as they gave
me.

Thank you for your endless support, your
enduring love, and for being there throughout
this journey.

———————————

Songlist

Click here - _Spotify_

I Would Die For You – Miley Cyrus
Kiss Me – Ed Sheeran
Head Above Water – Avril Lavigne
Don't Give Up On Me – Andy Grammer
Moon Shines Red – Jamie McDell
Scars – James Bay
Until The End – Quietdrive
Edge of the Dark – Armon Jay
Look Away – Eli Lieb, Steve Grand
You Said You'd Grow Old With Me – Michael Schulte
Tightrope – Ron Pope
Till the World Stops Turning – Kaleb Jones
My Life With You – Ryan Star
Element – Matthew Mayfield
Our Song – Ron Pope
When I Look At You – Miley Cyrus
Welcome Home – Radical Face

Synopsis

I had my life all planned out.
At twenty-eight, I'd meet my prince.
At thirty, we'd get married.
At thirty-two, we'd have a child.

How does that saying go about best-laid plans?

Here I am at thirty-two. Miserable, alone, and running out of time.

Then my prince arrives. I didn't expect he would be Ryker West.

But it turns out just like death, love comes when you least expect it.

Danny, Danny, quite contrary
Why doesn't your hair grow?
With IVs and pain,
And death waiting to take the final blow.

Forbidden Heir

THE HEIRS
Book 8

*Contemporary Romance in The Heirs series.
As it's the final book, it will be better understood
after all the other books have been read.*

"All we have to decide is what to do with the time that is given us." — *J. R. R Tolkien.*

Family Tree

DANNY (DANIELE) HAYES

↓ ↓

Carter Hayes | Della Truman
Father | *Mother*

Godmother: Jamie Truman

Godfather: Rhett Daniels

RYKER WEST

↓ ↓

Logan West | Mia Daniels
Father | *Mother*

Godmother: Leigh Baxter

Godfather: Jaxson West

Best friend: Tristan Hayes

Danny, Danny, quite contrary
Why doesn't your hair grow?
With IVs and pain,
And death waiting to take the final blow.

Chapter 1

DANNY

Danny 32; Ryker 25

I'm lucky.

I have a loving and supportive family.

I have two brothers who would kill for me.

I have a big group of friends, even though they're all younger than me.

I'm the COO and chairperson of a multi-billion dollar company.

I'm my father's little girl.

I'm my godfather's princess.

I'm lucky.

Letting out a sigh, I look at my reflection in the mirror. The blue bridesmaid dress is gorgeous, and I'm happy for Christopher and Dash. They deserve their happily-ever-after. But the sight breaks my heart.

I'm thirty-two, and there's no sign of my prince. My youngest brother, Tristan, got married a year ago. My other brother, Christopher, is getting married in six weeks.

Damn, everyone I know is settling down. Getting married. Having children.

Everyone but me.

The one thing I've wanted most in life keeps eluding me.

Well… kind of. There is a man I'm interested in, but he's off-limits Like way off-limits.

Walking back to the dressing room, I carefully remove the dress and place it back on the hanger before putting on my suit. I fix my brown curls and put on some lipgloss, then force a smile around my mouth.

Time to get back to the office.

I thank the designer and walk out to my car. On the drive back to Indie Ink, the company started by my grandfather, I push my elusive dream deep down and slip into the role of Danny, the powerhouse businesswoman.

That's what my life consists of. Roles. Loving daughter. Loyal friend. Supportive sister. Kickass businesswoman.

Letting out a sigh, I park my car in the designated spot. I climb out of the vehicle, and squaring my shoulders, I walk to the elevator. Once inside, I press the button for the top floor and listen to the soft music until the doors slide open. Stepping out, I walk to my office.

"How did the fitting go?" Dash, my sister-in-law to be, asks before I can pass by her office.

Smiling, I inject excitement into my voice. "The dress is gorgeous and ready for your big day."

Dash claps her hands. "Just six more weeks."

"It's going to be amazing," I chuckle, and then I slip into my office. Shutting the door, I lean back against it. I close my eyes and take a deep breath.

"You look tired," Ryker suddenly says.

My eyes snap open, and seeing him in my chair, makes a wave of tingles rush over my skin.

Ryker West. My secret love.

Faking a scowl, I say, "Give me a heart attack next time." I walk toward my desk, my frown deepening. "Get out of my chair."

He grins at me while swiveling in the chair like a kid. "I'm here so we can go over all the files we need to take with us for the meeting." His eyes lock with mine. "You know… for the trip to Africa…" His mouth curves into a sexy smirk. "Where it will just be the two of us."

Ryker is my youngest brother's best friend and also the company's attorney. Since he started working at Indie Ink, taking over his father's position in the company, he's been doing his best to drive me insane.

It's like there's a constant push and pull between us. I do my best to ignore it, seeing as I'm six years older than him. Technically, I'm six and a half years older than him. The point is he's off-limits, so it's a constant battle to fight my feelings for him.

I stop next to the chair and let out a sigh. "I have last-minute business to take care of. We can look at the files later. Move."

Ryker gets up, and rising to his full height, I have to tilt my head back to keep eye contact with him. With dark brown hair, warm brown eyes, and a face carved from whatever precious stone they have in heaven, Ryker is ruggedly handsome.

And off-limits. Like the forbidden fruit reincarnated into a hot-as-hell man to tempt the ever-loving shit out of me.

Actually, I started feeling the attraction between us when Ryker was a senior in high school. *Yeah, totally made me feel like a perv.* There I was, twenty-five and drooling over Tristan's best friend. But damn, at eighteen, Ryker didn't look like any other senior I've ever seen. He's always been way too attractive for my ovaries to handle.

Ryker's smirk turns downright sinful, causing flutters to burst to life in my stomach. Then he murmurs, "You have ten minutes to hand over all your work to Christopher. The flight is tonight, so there's no putting this off until later."

I should get an award for my acting skills. I've mastered the art of hiding my true feelings from him.

Narrowing my eyes at him, I say, "You're giving me orders now?"

He lets out a chuckle. "Do you know tiny sparks explode in your eyes when I push your buttons?"

That's not the only place I get sparks.

I push by him and sit down. Turning to my desk, I pull a folder closer and open it.

Ryker places a hand on the back of my chair and another on my desk, and then he leans down until his face is right next to mine, and his cologne fills the air I breathe.

Good God, he smells fantastic.

14

I close my eyes and take a deep breath, hoping to all that's holy, I look irritated and not affected by him being so close to me.

"Ryker," I whisper, my resolve starting to slip.

You can't, Danny. It would make you a freaking cougar. Don't... just don't.

"Yes, Ma'am?" he murmurs, his voice low and deep by my ear, and I almost let out a need-filled groan.

"You're a second away from being demoted to a janitor," I threaten as my body starts to tremble with desire.

Ryker lets out another chuckle, and then he grabs the folder away from me and walks toward the door.

"Bring that back," I gasp.

"I'm giving it to Christopher. Get your ass to the round table so we can look over the files. I'm sure you still need to pack as well."

I stare at Ryker's broad back and then shake my head.

God, the business trip to South Africa is probably going to kill me. Three weeks alone with Ryker. The odds of surviving are not in my favor.

I'll probably die from my ovaries combusting.

A smile tugs at my mouth. Ryker West might be forbidden, but at the end of the day, when all is said and done, I live for these moments between us.

RYKER

We still have nine hours left before we'll land at Cape Town International. I watch Danny where she's sitting across from me on the company's private jet. Her eyes keep drifting shut before she's jarred awake again.

When her eyes close again, I get up from my seat. The second I slip my arms behind her back, and under her knees, she startles awake.

"What are you doing?" she mumbles.

"Putting you to bed," I murmur as I lift her to my chest.

When she doesn't fight me, it just tells me how exhausted she is.

Danny usually fights me on everything.

My mouth curves up from the thought.

Stepping inside the bedroom, I walk to the side of the bed, then lay Danny down on the white bedspread. When I glance at her face, I see that she's out cold. I remove her shoes, setting them down on the floor. Pulling the covers back on the other side of the mattress, I move Danny over and cover her.

I kick off my own shoes before I climb under the covers. Turning onto my side, I let my eyes drift over her face.

Danielle Hayes. Unattainable like the stars. Untouchable like the sun.

I've always loved Danny in some way. At first, she was my best friend's older sister with a beautiful smile and eyes as blue as the sky, who drove us to school and pretty much anywhere else we needed to go.

Then my balls dropped, and I noticed how smoking hot she was, especially during summer breaks. Seeing Danny in a bikini was the highlight of my teenage years.

But watching her run a company as big as Indie Ink – effortlessly, gracefully, never backing down – it's a constant turn-on.

Danny mumbles something as she turns over until she's facing me. Her button nose twitches, drawing a smile from me.

God, she's beautiful.

I push my left arm under the pillow, and it's just in time because Danny moves again, snuggling up against me. My body freezes as I watch her rub her cheek against my chest, and then my eyes drift shut from how good it feels to have her so close to me.

Praying she doesn't wake up because she will kick my ass and send me flying without a parachute, I carefully wrap my right arm around her.

Thank God she doesn't wake up, and I push my luck as I lower my head, pressing a kiss to her hair.

Damn, she smells good.

I take a deep breath of her soft scent.

Apples.

Danny is everything I want but can never have. I have to settle for flirting with her because I'm dead sure she only sees me as her little brother's friend.

God, sometimes life is just unfair.

Slowly, I tighten my arm around her, keeping my mouth pressed to her silky strands.

Loving Danny is both the hardest and easiest thing I've ever done. It's like the air I breathe, a necessity. And it's frustrating as fuck.

We've hugged before. Cheek kisses at Christmas and birthdays.

But I've never gotten to hold her like this, and it's overwhelming. Getting a taste of the only thing I want in this life, knowing this might be it – all I'll ever get – is gutting.

Fuck, I love her.

Feeling her body against mine. Hearing her soft breaths. It creates a sweet ache in me.

I wish we could live in an alternate universe where we'd meet as strangers. She'd fall in love with me, because let's face it, I'm a good guy with a great sense of humor. I'd sweep her feet from under her.

I'd be the man who gets to make love to her.

I'd be the man to comfort her, her shoulder to rest her head on.

I'd be the man to change her last name.

I'd be the father of her children.

God. God. God. I want that dream so desperately.

My heart physically aches from knowing it will never happen.

Danny will never see me as anything more than Tristan's best friend.

Moving my hand up under her hair until I reach her neck, I soak in the feel of her soft skin. Danny presses closer to me, making me freeze again. My heartbeat begins to speed up as she pulls her arm from where it's between us, and she wraps it around my waist.

There's a painful twinge in my chest.

I want more of this. So much more.

I savor every second. I drink it in like a man dying of thirst. Danny's my mirage in the desert that's my life.

Chapter 2

DANNY

Taking a seat on a plush couch, my eyes follow Ryker to the reception, where he'll get our keycards and room numbers.

At least he got an international driver's license and rented a car so we can get around without having to be dependent on South African public transport, that's apparently not trustworthy.

I'm still flustered from waking up glued against his chest, our arms wrapped around each other. Of course, I didn't move a muscle, not wanting to wake him.

God, it felt so good being held by the man I love.

My eyes drift over his back, his trim waist, and his butt… damn, carved from steel.

Just remembering his arm tightening around me and his breath on my hair has my body warming until I'm pretty sure I'm close to reaching spontaneous-combustion level.

When he turns around and heads back to me, his steps are confident... filled with strength. I let out a needy sigh and get up as he reaches me.

"We're sharing," he states.

"What?" I blink at him like an idiot.

The corner of his mouth lifts. "The penthouse. It has two bedrooms so you can relax."

"Oh... good," I mutter as I take hold of my luggage handle. Pulling the bag behind me, I walk toward the elevator.

We'll be staying at The Silo. It's a five-star hotel built on top of Africa's largest museum of contemporary art. It's also situated in the heart of the waterfront, which I'm excited to explore at some point during our stay here.

When we walk into the suite, I glance around at the living and dining area. The view of the Atlantic Ocean is gorgeous.

"Is that Robben Island?" I ask.

"Yes. We can plan a day trip if you want to visit it," Ryker says. He glances inside the bedrooms, then asks, "Which one do you want?"

I walk to the first one, saying, "It doesn't matter. I won't be doing much sleeping."

"Just as well you slept on the plane." Hearing the teasing note in his voice, I shoot him a glare before shutting the door behind me.

Taking black slacks, a white blouse, and underwear from my bag, I head to the luxurious bathroom. I run myself a bubble bath and soak a good ten minutes in the aromatic water.

In five days, we're meeting with the board of Take3, South Africa's largest eCommerce store. Either we'll agree to a partnership, or we'll have to start from scratch and become competition for them.

The latter means there will be a couple of trips from the states to South Africa in the future. Our foothold here will secure us the continent.

Climbing out of the tub. I dry myself and lather my body in lotion. I'll visit the hotel's hairdresser to get my hair taken care of because it's the last thing I have the energy for now.

I tie the strands up in a ponytail, and once I'm dressed, I walk out into the shared living space.

"Ryker," I call out.

"Yes, ma'am?" His muted answer comes from his bedroom. Hearing him call me ma'am makes my lips curve up.

Damn, it's such a turn-on.

Clearing my throat, I say, "I need the files and laptops."

"Come get it."

Taking a deep breath, I push the door open, and not seeing Ryker, I walk to where the leather briefcase and laptop bags are. Just as I pick them up, Ryker comes out of the bathroom with only a fluffy white towel wrapped low around his waist.

Dear God.

My mouth drops open, and my eyes widen. Not from shock, but to get a better view.

Wow.

Holy mother of abs.

Ryker's mouth instantly curves up into the sinful smirk, I usually either want to slap or kiss off his face. Right now, it's the latter.

My gaze rakes hungrily over his chiseled chest and abs before getting stuck on the fuck-me muscles, which point a direct arrow into the towel.

Fall off. Fall off. Fall off.

"See something you like?" Ryker asks, bursting my lust-induced bubble.

Letting out a disgruntled huff as a reply, I leave his room as quickly as I can. Feeling frazzled, I plop down on a couch and open the briefcase. I take out the files and spread them over the coffee table.

Focus, Danny. On work, not Ryker.

RYKER

I stare at the door where Danny just rushed through.

That was definitely interest I saw on her face. I'm not that far gone that I'm imagining things. Right?

Just as well she left so quickly. A second longer of her staring at me like that, and she would've had a front-row seat to me sporting a hard-on.

Grabbing a pair of jeans and a black t-shirt, I get changed before walking out of the room.

Danny glances up, then asks, "Did you bring the financials Noah prepared?"

I head to the coffee table and scan over the files. Picking up the one clearly marked 'Financials,' I hold it out to her.

"Oh… thanks."

"Scoot over," I murmur, and when she does, I sit down next to her.

When she opens the file, I lean closer to see, and then we get to work. After an hour, I lift my arm and rest it on the back of the couch. It has my body pressing close to Danny's.

"Take3's worth is fifteen billion, right?" I ask.

"Uh-huh," Danny mumbles.

I reach for one of the pages in the file and feel Danny tensing. My eyes dart to her face. Her lips are parted, and her lashes lowered. She takes a deep breath, then lifts her gaze to mine.

The intense pull I always feel around her starts to grow until it's impossible for me to focus on anything else.

All I have to do is lean in and take the one thing I've always wanted.

When she doesn't say anything but just keeps looking at me, it makes my heartbeat speed up.

God, what if?

My mind's still contemplating shit when my body begins to slowly lean into her.

Danny's breaths start to come faster, and it makes the corner of my mouth curve up.

Before I can kiss her, her phone begins to ring, and it shreds right through the anticipation that was building between us.

Danny darts up and drops the file on the table before she answers the call. "Yes, James."

Knowing it's her PA, I grab my laptop and open it. She'll be on that call for a while, so I might as well get back to work.

I open the proposal I'm setting up but stare at it as my thoughts turn to what just happened.

The attraction can't possibly just be one-sided. Danny reacted. Right? It's not like she moved away from me or told me to focus on the financials. Her eyes were locked on mine. I was a couple of seconds away from kissing her, and she didn't move a muscle to stop me.

My eyes lift to where Danny's pacing up and down on the other side of the room.

She glances at me but instantly looks away when she sees I'm watching her.

Holy fuck. Maybe she doesn't only see me as Tristan's best friend?

I have three weeks with her in Cape Town. Maybe this is my chance?

My heart begins to pound against my ribs with excitement as I lower my gaze back to my laptop's screen.

Okay, don't rush, Ryker. Be calm. Take things slowly. You can't afford to fuck things up. Up your flirting game and see how she responds.

My heart keeps racing as I try to focus on the work.

Danny stays on the call for an hour, and the moment she hangs up, I ask, "Do you want to order in or go to the restaurant for dinner?"

She drops down on the couch and leans back. Rubbing her temple, she says, "Order in, please."

There's a flash of pain on her face, and it has a frown forming on my forehead. "You okay?"

"Yeah, just a headache." She drops her phone on the table as she gets up again. "Probably from the long flight."

"I'll get you something." Rising to my feet, I walk to my room and put on shoes before grabbing my wallet, the car keys, and the keycard for the hotel room. When I head out again, I notice Danny's gone to her bedroom. Tapping on the door, I push it open. She's curled up at the foot end of the bed. I move closer and ask, "What do you feel like eating?"

"Something small. A sandwich," she mumbles.

"Is it just a headache?"

She wouldn't fake it because I made her uncomfortable. Right?

Danny nods. "I'll just nap for an hour, then we can get back to work."

"Okay." My eyes drift over her before I turn and leave the suite.

I go to the concierge and ask, "Where's the nearest drug store?"

The woman blinks all shocked at me, then asks, "Oh, you mean a pharmacy?"

"Yes."

She gives me directions, and at least it's not too far away. Getting painkillers is an experience, but I manage to get something for Danny's headache. The sandwiches I get from a local store.

By the time I get back to the hotel, it's already past six. I walk to Danny's room, and seeing she's awake, I say, "Food and then painkillers."

"Thanks." She gets up, looking a little out of it.

I wait for her to sit down in the living room, then hand her a sandwich before I grab a water from the fridge for each of us.

We eat our sandwiches in silence, and I make sure Danny takes two painkillers before we get back to work.

Four hours later, my phone begins to ring, and seeing it's Christopher, I answer, "Missing us already?"

"Yeah. Where's the Sutherland contract?" he asks.

"Did you ask Dorris?" I handed everything to my assistant before I left.

"She's out on lunch."

"I left everything with her," I say.

"I'll wait for her to get back. How was the flight?" he asks.

"As good as a twenty-nine-hour flight can be," I chuckle.

"What's the time there?"

I check my watch. "Just shy of ten pm."

"Shit, go get some rest," Christopher mutters, then he adds, "Make sure my sister sleeps."

"Will do."

Ending the call, I glance at Danny. She's pressing two fingers against her temple, and it has me saying. "Let's call it a night. We can get an early start tomorrow morning."

When she nods, my eyebrow raises, and I can't resist teasing her. "What? No, go to hell, Ryker. I'm going to work myself to a standstill?"

She lets out a huff, then mutters, "I'm too tired to care right now."

Danny walks to her bedroom, and before she closes the door, she says, "Night."

"Night." I stare at the closed door for a moment, then turn my attention back to the files.

Chapter 3

DANNY

When I wake up, my thoughts instantly return to the night before.

A frown forms on my forehead as I turn onto my side, staring out the expansive bay windows at the rising sun.

What happened last night? Was it just my overactive imagination? I replay the almost kiss, trying to figure out if it was real or just wishful thinking.

Ryker placing his arm on the back of the couch. His body pressing against mine. That look.

God, that look.

I felt it in my ovaries, and it froze me in place.

He leaned in. I'm sure of it.

Shit! Does he know I have a crush on him, and he's just teasing me?

Would Ryker do something like that?

No, not the Ryker I know. He'd never play with someone's emotions.

But he leaned in as if he was going to kiss me.

My frown deepens, and it feels like I'm trying to put together a puzzle with only half the pieces.

Letting out a frustrated sigh, I get up and walk to my bathroom so I can get ready for the day.

Then again… there's no way Ryker has romantic feelings toward me. I mean, shit, I'm almost seven years older than him. He probably sees me as an older sister.

I pull a disgruntled face as I brush my teeth.

Maybe there was a smudge or an eyelash or something on my face? Hell if I know.

I let out another sigh and rinse my mouth.

I finish my morning routine and put on a pair of jeans and a cream blouse. Leaving my room, my eyes instantly go to Ryker's closed door. I prepare myself a cup of coffee, then leaning back against the counter, I slowly sip the warm liquid.

Shit, was it really just my imagination?

Ryker's door opens, and then my eyebrows pop up as I bring the mug to my parting lips.

He's only wearing grey sweatpants, and they're hanging low on his hips. Greedily my eyes rake over his chest and abs. And those damn curves by his hips that reduce my IQ to zero.

My abdomen tightens as I watch his muscles ripple beneath his tanned skin. Then my gaze gets stuck on the bulge. If that's the outline, then I'd love to see the real thing.

Ryker stops next to me to make himself a cup of coffee, then he murmurs, "Morning." His voice sounds low and rough, and it makes desire burn through my body.

Somehow, I manage to mumble, "Morning."

Some brain activity returns, enough for me to remember my own coffee. I take a sip, and unable to stop myself, my head slowly turns, and then my eyes are feasting on his body again.

Damn, his arm, the veins, the... everything.

When Ryker's done preparing his coffee, he turns to face me, leaning his hip against the counter. He takes a sip, his eyes locking on my face.

He just watches me as he drinks his coffee, and it has my heartbeat speeding up until I'm sure he can either hear the crazy pounding in my chest or see my pulse fluttering like a caged bird.

"We need to work on the proposal today," I say just for the sake of saying something.

"Yes, ma'am," his voice rumbles.

It hits me square in the ovaries, and before I can stop myself, my eyes drift closed, and I let out a needy breath. I try to hide my reaction behind my cup as I take another sip of my coffee.

"Did you sleep okay?" he asks.

Opening my eyes, I nod, but I have to clear my throat before I ask, "And you?"

"Not too bad." Ryker reaches for my face, and it has me freezing. I feel his finger brush over my earlobe and down my neck, then he murmurs, "You had some hair stuck on your earring."

"Thanks," I practically squeak, my voice throwing a disappearing act because I'm overwhelmed by the tingles his touch gave me.

"How's the headache?" he asks, sipping on the rest of his coffee.

Headache?

It takes a moment for me to remember. "Oh, it's gone."

"Good." The low rumble almost draws a moan from me.

God, his voice alone is pure sex.

I set the empty mug down, but I can't bring myself to move away from him.

Come on, Danny. You're only going to embarrass yourself. You're thirty-two, not some love-struck teenager.

"We should get to work," I whisper as I force myself to walk toward the living room. Sitting down on the couch, I take a deep breath and let it out slowly.

This is going to be one hell of a long business trip. Fighting my attraction toward Ryker is becoming an impossible struggle.

Ryker goes back to his room, and minutes later, he comes out wearing a pair of jeans and a white t-shirt that spans tight around his biceps.

Not much better than the sweatpants. He still looks hot as hell.

He sits down next to me, and picking up his laptop, he brings it to his lap. I grab my own device and settle back against the couch as I open it.

Then Ryker leans back, and his arm and leg press against mine. I get a whiff of his cologne.

Damn, he always smells good.

He probably doesn't even realize our bodies are touching. I watch as he opens the document containing the proposal, and then my eyes drop to his hand as he begins to scroll up.

I wonder what it would feel like to have his hands on me. I'd probably orgasm in less than a minute.

My skin flushes from the thought, and it has me shifting on the couch, only making me more aware of his body pressing against mine.

I'm not going to get any work done at this rate. Trying to focus on the proposal, I say, "Make sure there's no way for them to have any claim to Indie Ink if we sign a deal."

"Yes, ma'am," he murmurs.

Another burst of heat spreads through me, but I force myself to narrow my eyes at him. "Stop calling me ma'am."

Because it only makes me want you more, and I'm hanging on by a thin thread as is.

His lips curve up into the sinful smirk I love so much, and then his eyes flick to mine. "You love when I call you ma'am."

His statement has my eyes narrowing more.

Does he know how I feel about him?

Shit, if that's the case, I might as well just die of mortification because there's no way I'll live it off.

"Yeah, so much that I'm going to demote your butt if you keep calling me that," I mutter, trying to cover up my emotions, just in case. I move up, putting some space between us, and then I focus on my work.

RYKER

I keep getting mixed signals from Danny, and it only frustrates me more.

This morning she checked me out. Like all of me. There was definitely a moment where her eyes dropped down to my cock.

Now she's scowling at me and putting space between us?

Fuck, I don't know if it's just my imagination. Do I want this so much, I'm starting to see things that aren't there?

"Are you clued up on all the countries' different business laws?" Danny asks.

"Yeah, at least the ones we're looking at in Africa," I answer.

"We should focus on South Africa's neighboring countries. From what I've read, it's easy to import and export between them."

"Yes, ma'am," I mutter.

Danny lets out a huff, then she starts looking at Botswana's economy.

An hour later, hunger begins to gnaw at my insides. "Time for breakfast," I say as I shut my laptop.

"Already?" Danny asks as she glances at her watch.

"Yes, or you won't get shit out of me today. I need food unlike you," I grumble as I get up.

"I eat," she mutters.

"Put on your shoes," I order as I walk to my room to get my own.

Danny doesn't argue, which I'm thankful for. After only having breakfast on the plane and the sandwich for dinner yesterday, I could eat half a cow.

I grab my wallet, the keycard, and car keys, then walk back into the living room.

Danny comes out of her room, asking, "You're paying, right? Then I don't have to take my bag."

"Sure."

"Are we eating in the hotel or taking a walk?" Danny asks.

I let out a chuckle. "We won't be taking any walks while we're here."

Her eyes dart to mine. "Why not?"

"Because it's dangerous, Danny. Cape Town is, after all, ranked as the most murderous city in the world." My lips curve up. "Which means you go nowhere without me."

Luckily, she doesn't argue with me. "So, are we eating here or going out?"

"There's a mall nearby. Let's see if we can find a breakfast place there." Instantly she smiles, and it has me adding, "Let me know if there's a place you want to visit."

"I was really hoping we could take a wine tour before we go home."

"I'll check. Maybe we can go on one this weekend." Not that I drink alcohol, but if it's something Danny wants to do, I'll make it happen.

"That will be great."

We walk to the front door, and as we leave, I place my hand on Danny's lower back. She doesn't scowl at me or comment about it.

It's a short drive to the mall, but damn, there are minibuses, which are used as cabs, everywhere. It feels as if I'm doing an advanced driving course as I maneuver the car between them.

"Ryker!" Danny gasps, and she grabs hold of my thigh when one of the minibuses suddenly swerves in front of us, coming to a stop in the middle of the road.

I slam on the breaks, and then we have to wait for them to offload passengers before we're moving again.

"Welcome to Africa," I mutter, highly conscious of Danny's hand on my thigh. Every couple of seconds, her grip on me tightens when a car passes close by us.

We make it to the mall in one piece, and as I park the car, Danny lets out a breath of relief.

I lower my hand to hers and give her a squeeze. "You okay?"

"Yeah, but... damn... don't these people know how to drive?"

"Apparently not." I give her hand another squeeze. "Let's find a place to eat."

I get out of the car and walk around to the passenger side. Opening the door, I take hold of Danny's hand as she climbs out.

We're approached by a man, and it has Danny ducking behind me.

"Can I wash your car?"

"No, thanks," I mutter as I pull Danny to my right side. She sticks close to me, and her hand tightens on mine. It has me linking our fingers as we walk toward an entrance.

We find a restaurant called Mugg & Bean that looks decent, and reaching the table, I let go of Danny's hand as I pull her chair out.

"Thank God," she mumbles under her breath.

Taking a seat next to her, I ask, "When's the last time you traveled?"

She glances around. "With my parents for my twenty-first birthday. We went to Croatia, and it was nothing like this."

Raising my eyebrow, I ask, "Seriously? Didn't you go on a business trip..." I have to think when it was, "four years ago?"

"That was to Canada."

Shaking my head, my eyes lock on hers. "You don't take vacations, do you?"

Danny grins at me. "Work keeps me busy."

"Too busy," I mutter as a waiter brings our menus. We both settle for cappuccinos then the waiter leaves us to look over the selection of meals.

Danny lets out a chuckle. "They have California omelet, which reminds me nothing of home."

After discussing the menu, Danny decides on a classic breakfast while I choose the South African farm one. I hope that plate is loaded.

Once we have our cappuccinos, Danny gives me an apologetic look. "Sorry for clinging to you."

My lips instantly curve up. "I don't mind."

Our eyes lock for a moment too long, and it has Danny shifting on her chair as she glances around us again.

While we wait for our food to come, we listen to the different languages being spoken. It's fascinating, but my attention soon drifts back to Danny.

Seeing her out of her comfort zone shows me a whole new side to her. She's always calm and collected. The businesswoman who can make any man bend to her will.

But right now, she looks vulnerable, and it makes my protective side rear to life.

Danny begins to frown, and then she says, "Maybe we should get a security team."

Her gaze meets mine when I shake my head. "That will draw attention to us. It's the last thing we want to do. Just blend in."

Danny's eyes darts around us. "Easier said than done."

Reaching for her hand, I wrap my fingers over hers. "I won't let anything happen to you."

Her lips instantly curve up, and then she murmurs, "Hmm… my personal bodyguard?"

I let out a chuckle. "Amongst other things."

I don't let go of her hand, and it has Danny glancing down, then she asks, "Like?"

Our eyes meet again as I say, "Whatever you need me to be."

For a moment, she just stares at me, but before she can comment on what I said, our food comes, and I have to let go of her.

Chapter 4

DANNY

We've been here three days, and with every passing hour, it becomes more challenging to focus on my work.

Ryker consumes my thoughts. His cologne is everywhere, and it's beginning to feel as if I'm high on the masculine scent.

And the touching. God, the touching.

His hand on my lower back. His thigh pressing against mine. Whenever he takes hold of my hand.

All the touching is driving me wild with desire.

I'm standing out on the balcony, staring at the dark blue ocean while I try to regain control over my emotions for the hundredth time.

This is torture.

I close my eyes against the stab of heartache. Not being able to have Ryker might just kill me. I don't know what I'll do when he settles down with another woman. It's only a matter of time, though.

I feel Ryker's hand on my back, and it has my eyes snapping open. He comes to stand really close to me, showing me his cellphone's screen, and once again, I feel overwhelmed from having him near me.

"There are two wine tours. Take a look and let me know which one you want to go on."

"Thanks." I take the phone from him and scroll through the tours. Knowing I'm going to butcher the word if I try to pronounce it, I point at the second tour. "This one looks good."

Ryker glances over the information, then he says, "Great, we can go on Saturday."

A smile spreads over my face. "Thank you." I follow him back to the living room, and while Ryker secures our tickets for the tour, I force my attention back to my work. The meeting is tomorrow, and even though I feel prepared, I have an obsession with checking and rechecking everything.

When Ryker's done, I say, "Can we go over the proposal one more time?"

"Sure." He moves closer to me as he flips his laptop open on the coffee table in front of us. Every time he has to scroll down, his elbow rests on my knee, and after the fifth page, he doesn't pull back.

Don't read anything into it, Danny. He's just comfortable with you. Nothing's going on.

I focus on the screen and then say, "Clause four-point-one. Is it really needed?"

"Which one?" Ryker asks, and it has me leaning forward so I can point it out on the screen. The moment my left breast presses against his arm, my eyebrows shoot up.

"Ah… the… uhm," I begin to stammer, and then I dart back against the couch. "Four-point-one," I finally get it out.

Ryker glances back at me, a scrutinizing expression sharpening his eyes.

Oh God. He picked up on that.

I get up and walk to the fridge to grab a bottle of water. I take a couple of sips while I collect myself… again.

When I turn around, it's only to find Ryker watching me, then he asks, "Are you okay?"

Time for another Oscar-worthy performance, Danny.

I let out a chuckle. "Yeah, of course. Why would you ask that?"

He shrugs, then turns his attention back to the laptop. "No reason."

I drink some more water and take deep breaths to calm down my racing heart. Once I feel more in control of my hormones and emotions, I walk back to the couch and sit down again, leaving enough space between us to fit another person.

I actually manage to get work done after that and only glance up from my laptop when a light goes on in the living room. "Is it that late already?"

"Yep, which means it's time for a break," Ryker replies. He walks to his room, and then the door shuts behind him.

Knowing he must be hungry, I place an order for two steaks before I go to my own room so I can relax in a bath.

I let the water into the tub then strip out of my clothes. As I climb into the tub, I let out a sigh at how amazing the water feels.

I soak for a little while, but knowing they'll deliver our food soon, I quickly wash then climb out. I let the water drain then dry myself. Opening the bathroom door so I can grab clothes, I freeze when my bedroom door opens.

"Danny, did you order –" Ryker's words cut off as his gaze swoops over my body.

I slam the bathroom door shut then stare at it.

Oh. My. God.

Ryker just saw me butt naked.

My hand flies to my mouth as my eyes widen.

Nooooooo.

"I didn't see anything," he calls out. "Well, not much."

My mouth drops open as I glare at the door.

"Leave!" I yell at him.

I hear the bedroom door shut, and slowly, I open the bathroom door, peeking into the room. Not seeing Ryker, I run for my closet and yank clothes out. I hurry to put on my underwear, sweatpants, a t-shirt, and even though it's summer here, a freaking sweater. I try to cover as much skin as possible, and then I sit down on the side of the bed.

Ugh... Ryker saw me naked.

I cover my face with my hands and take a couple of deep breaths.

It's okay. You'll survive this. Somehow.

Knowing I have to face him at some point, I let out a sulking sound. Getting up, I walk to the door. I yank it open and send Ryker a scowl where he's standing by the dining table.

"Sorry, I wanted to ask if you ordered food," he says, the corner of his mouth lifting.

Locking eyes with him, I threaten, "If you tell a single soul, I will smother you in our sleep."

He lets out a chuckle, and it makes my face flame up. The love of my life just saw me naked, and now he's laughing.

Wow… just wow.

Shaking my head, I turn around and walk back to my room. I'm not emotionally equipped to deal with this right now.

RYKER

Fuck. Fuck. Fuck.

Darting after Danny, I take hold of her arm, but it only has her yanking away from me. I get a glimpse of her face, and seeing the hurt expression makes me feel like shit.

I grab hold of her wrist, and this time, I yank her to me. Folding my arms around her, I say, "I'm sorry. I wanted to ease the tension. I wasn't laughing at you."

"Could've fooled me," she mumbles.

I tighten my arms around her, and not thinking, I press a kiss to the side of her head. "I'm sorry, Danny. It was an accident. I knocked, and you didn't answer. I thought you were taking a nap."

"Can we not talk about the most embarrassing moment of my life?" she mutters against my chest.

I hate that she's embarrassed. God, with a body like hers… the memory of her breasts, her toned stomach, her hips and… I begin to harden and instantly pull away from her.

"Deal," I answer her as I walk to the dining table. I sit down to hide my hard as fuck dick, then gesture at the other plate of food. "Let's eat."

She comes to sit down but refuses to look at me.

Leaning back in the chair, I ask, "Will you feel better if I strip? That way, we're even."

Her eyes fly to my face, and tilting her head, it actually looks like she's considering my offer.

I get up, and grabbing hold of the shirt at the back of my neck, I pull it off.

Danny leans her elbows on the table and rests her chin in her palm, but the moment my thumbs slip into my waistband, she lets out a chuckle. "Stop."

"I don't mind," I say, the corner of my mouth lifting.

"I'm sure you don't," she mutters as she takes the lid off her plate. "You have nothing to hide."

Dragging my shirt back on, I sit down. "You have nothing to hide either." I pick up my cutlery. "Nothing at all."

"Not making me feel better," she mumbles as she cuts into her steak.

I hate that she's uncomfortable, so I keep going, "You're beautiful, Danny."

She makes a strangled sound in the back of her throat, her eyes snapping to me.

I hold her gaze. "I'm not just saying it because we're friends. I mean it."

"Thanks. Can we leave it now?"

"I don't want you to be uncomfortable," I admit.

"I'll survive." She takes a bite then focuses on her food.

I take a couple of bites while my eyes keep darting to her.

It's impossible to forget what I saw. Danny's… perfect.

When she catches me staring at her, she lets out a sigh. "You're making it worse."

"Sorry," I murmur, but then I figure I might as well be honest with her. "But you have one hell of a hot body."

Danny takes a deep breath as she sets her cutlery down, then her eyes lock on mine. "You're really not going to let it go?"

"Kind of hard." Pun intended.

Danny's not stupid, far from. Her gaze lowers to my lap before returning to my face. She picks up her cutlery again, then mutters, "Eat so we can get back to work."

"Yes, ma'am," I murmur, and I don't miss how the corner of her mouth lifts.

Then it hits me. Danny wasn't pissed off that I saw her naked. She was embarrassed. If Tristan had walked in on her, she would've slapped him upside the head.

My eyes sharpen on her. The faint blush on her cheeks.

Holy shit.

Danny glances up, then she frowns. "What?"

"Nothing," I answer quickly. *Yet.*

But if my gut is right…

Chapter 5

DANNY

The first meeting with Take3 went much better than I expected. We've already been in South Africa for six days, and all we've seen is the inside of the hotel room, Take3's offices, and that nerve-wracking trip to the mall.

Ryker's been working non-stop on the interim contract, where I've been doing further research on the market.

Dressed in a pair of shorts, a t-shirt, and sandals, I walk out of my bedroom.

Ryker glances in my direction as he comes out of his own room, then he stops and stares at me. "Damn, I can't remember when last I saw you in casual clothes."

Rolling my eyes, I ask, "Do you expect me to go to the beach in a suit?"

He lets out a burst of silent laughter. "I wouldn't be surprised if you did."

Scrunching my nose, I pick up my bag. "Let's go before I change my mind."

Not that I would. I'm looking forward to spending some time on the beach before going on the Franschhoek wine route tour for the day.

Leaving the hotel, Ryker drives us to the nearest accessible beach. He finds a parking space in a designated area, and then we have to follow a path through houses. The ocean is a deep blue, and honestly, it looks cold even though it's summer on this side of the planet.

When we reach the sand, I grab hold of Ryker's arm. "Give me a second." He helps me keep my balance while I slip off my sandals. "Thanks."

Due to the rocks, mountain and houses surrounding the beach, it feels like we're in a cove. With my eyes on the waves rushing to shore, I walk closer to the water.

"Gosh, it's pretty," I sigh, and then I let out a shriek when Ryker wraps an arm around my waist, and I'm lifted into the air. I drop my sandals as he carries me into the water, and it has me laughing. "No. Shit, it's cold. I'm going to kill you."

The second he lets go of me, I splash water his way before making an awkward run for the sand. I don't get far. Ryker grabs hold of me again and then drags me in deeper. "Dead…" I shiver. "So dead."

The only answer I get from him is laughter.

When I try to turn around in his hold, a wave washes our feet from under us, and then I'm tumbling and swallowing the salty water.

I manage to sit up, and then Ryker lets out a bark of laughter. "You look like the girl from The Ring."

I begin to cough and send him a scathing glare. A sharp pain shoots through my head, and my vision blurs. I let out a groan, and it has Ryker crouching in front of me. He takes hold of my shoulder and wipes the hair from my face. "Did you get hurt?"

I shake my head, and it has the sharp pain lessening to a dull ache. "Just a headache." I scowl up at him. "Probably from all the water I just swallowed."

Ryker helps me climb to my feet, then says, "We'll stop by the hotel to change, then you can take some painkillers."

The painkillers he got suck, but I'm not about to tell him that because then he'll start worrying.

Walking over the soft white sand, I say, "I'm going to plant my butt right here and soak up some sun. I'm sure it will go away soon."

I sit down and wiggle my toes in the sand. Ryker drops down beside me, and when his arm presses against mine, it sends a zap straight to my abdomen.

You'd think after all these years, I'd be used to those pesky zaps.

We sit in silence for a couple of minutes, and then I admit, "This is the first day I've taken off in a year... I think."

"You work too hard," Ryker grumbles.

"Someone has to."

My reply has him turning his face to me. "There are eight of us. You keep forgetting that."

"I know." I pull my legs to my chest and rest my chin on my knees.

"Do you?" Ryker asks. "Indie Ink won't fall apart without you."

His words cause a ripple of heartache to spread through me. Not that I want Indie Ink to fall apart without me, but it's all I have.

"Thanks for that vote of confidence," I mutter.

Ryker nudges at me with his shoulder. "You know that's not what I meant. You just need to take some time off like the rest of us."

"I'll rest when I'm dead," I chuckle.

RYKER

After stopping at the hotel for a change of clothes, I program the GPS, so we don't accidentally end up on the other side of the country.

It's an hour's drive to where the tour starts, and every now and then, I steal a glance at Danny. There's a constant soft smile playing around her lips as she watches the landscape pass us by.

Clearing my throat, I ask, "How are Christopher and Dash's wedding plans coming along?" I think it's great that Danny's brother is marrying my cousin.

Danny turns her face to me. "Good. Everything is pretty much planned."

"I'm glad they finally got together." Dash was kidnapped by a deranged ex-boyfriend a month and a half ago. We all lost our minds there for a week or two, but it looks like she's recovering. The thought sends a wave of anger through me. I don't know much of the details, but I'm sure Tristan took care of the fucker the same way he took care of the guy who attacked my little sister, Mila.

God, there are some vile men in the world.

I know people question Tristan's morals, but after all the shit that's happened, I've realized the world needs people like him to take out the trash. That's why I'll never judge my best friend, no matter what path he walks in life.

Danny's features tighten, and she quickly looks back out the window.

"You okay?"

She nods. "Yeah, just a little tired."

"Take a nap. I'll wake you when we get there," I offer.

She lets out a chuckle. "I'm fine."

Since I saw Danny naked and her response to it, I've been on a mission to find out where her head is at.

There's a moment's silence, then I ask, "So when are you planning on getting married?"

Danny makes a scoffing sound. "I'm happy with my cat."

"You have a cat?"

She lets out a chuckle. "Actually, no. Like I have the time to look after an animal."

Taking a deep breath, I ask, "So no prospective boyfriends?"

She shakes her head. "No."

Pushing my luck, I ask, "Aren't you dating?"

Danny turns her face back to me, frowning. "What's with the twenty questions?"

I try to look casual as I shrug. "Just making conversation."

"What about you?" she asks. "Have you met your future Mrs. West yet?"

A burst of laughter escapes me. "Yeah, she just doesn't know it yet," I joke.

Danny stares at me with an expression of shock. "Are you serious or joking?"

"Joking, of course," I mutter. "You keep me too busy at work for me to have any kind of relationship."

"I'm just saving all the women out there. If I give you half a second, you'd probably turn into the playboy of the year," she grumbles.

I raise an eyebrow at her. "Is that how you see me? A playboy?"

She shrugs. "You have the looks."

My lips curve up. "So, you think I'm attractive?"

Danny glares at me. "Do you really need me to stroke your ego?"

Before I can stop the words, they're out, "I can think of something else you can stroke."

Dead silence fills the car for a solid minute before I begin to laugh. "God, that came out wrong."

"You think?" Danny gasps.

"I'm sorry," I mutter through my laughter.

She turns her face away from me, staring at the landscape again. After ten long minutes, Danny says, "I was just joking. I don't think you're a playboy."

Yeah? So, what do you think?

It's on the tip of my tongue to ask, but I bite my bottom lip to keep it in.

"I think you're a solid guy, Ryker. You'll make someone very happy one day."

Hopefully, that someone will be you.

Danny wraps her arms around her waist and goes back to staring out the window.

Turning on the radio, I really don't care what's playing as long as it gets rid of the awkward silence.

This is what I don't get. The one minute we're fine, and the next, she shuts down.

God, it sucks. We're sitting in the same car, but she might as well be on the other side of the world.

When I finally pull up to where the tour starts, I let out a breath of relief. We get out of the car and stretch our bodies before I walk to the tram that will be stopping at the different farms.

I wait for Danny to get on and take a seat next to her. The sides of our bodies press against each other, and it makes my muscles tighten.

Torture. Sweet fucking torture.

The tram begins to move, and we enjoy the view of rustic stores before the scenery changes to vineyards.

"It's so pretty. Like a postcard picture," Danny murmurs, the soft smile back around her lips.

"Yeah," I whisper, my eyes on her.

We stop at the first farm, and getting off, Danny sticks to my side as we walk toward a barn. Vats of wine are the only décor, and the small group of tourists we're with gather around a huge wooden table.

The first glass we taste sends a shiver racing over my body. *God, that's bitter.* I've never been one for wine or any kind of alcohol, but here I am… for Danny.

"Hmm…" My gaze instantly darts to her face. "It has a smokey… woodsy taste."

She looks at me, and I let out a chuckle. "What you said."

By the time we get to the third farm, I'm starting to get worried. The wine is going straight to my head. There's no way I'll be able to drive us back to the hotel.

Taking hold of Danny's hand, I pull her to a stop. "I think we should look at getting a room for the night before we carry on with the tour."

Danny lets out a burst of sparkling laughter. "Are you feeling tipsy?"

Nodding, I pull my phone out and mutter, "Rather safe than sorry."

Chapter 6

DANNY

Oh God.

I'm struggling to walk in a straight line. Grabbing Ryker's arm, I try to keep myself balanced, but he's not much help.

"I'm going to face plant on the path," I laugh.

"It feels like I had an entire bottle of wine," he grumbles.

I let out a bark of laughter. "That's because you practically did."

We get to the guesthouse Ryker arranged for us. Just as well. I don't think we'll be able to get back to the car, never mind the hotel with the state we're in.

I watch as Ryker struggles to unlock the door and begin to laugh at him. "You're drunk."

"A little," he chuckles. "Okay, a lot."

We laugh as we enter the guesthouse, and I kick off my shoes. "I'm not tired."

Ryker walks to the TV and switches it on. He begins to scroll through all the music channels, and when he lands on something with a beat, I grab the remote from him and hold it hostage against my chest as I dance away from him.

A second later, I use the remote as a microphone, doing a god-awful job at lip-syncing. But who cares. I'm having fun.

The song comes to an end and when *Kiss Me* by Ed Sheeran comes on, I begin to sway, this time actually singing along.

Ryker stands rooted to the spot, just staring at me with that sinful smirk on his face… again.

I drop the remote, and tilting my head, I say, "One day, I'm either going to slap that smirk off your face or kiss you."

His eyebrow lifts, then he says, "I vote for the kiss."

A burst of laughter bubbles over my lips as I walk closer to him. "Stop smirking."

His lips only curve more as he shakes his head, his eyes darkening.

"That's it." Taking hold of his jaw, I struggle to lift myself on my toes without losing my balance and end up plastered against his chest. "Damn, you're too tall," I complain.

Ryker's eyes lock on mine as his hand settles on my back, keeping me pressed up against him. The smile fades from his face, and his eyes darken even more.

"Do you have any idea how hot you are?" I ask, my head filled with the happy buzz from all the wine.

Bringing his other hand to the side of my face, he begins to lean down until I can feel his breath on my lips.

It looks like he hesitates for a couple of seconds, and then his mouth is on mine, and I swear I hear fireworks going off in the distance.

There's also a siren, like a warning, but it's too vague for me to care when our tongues touch.

Ryker's hand slips behind my neck as he deepens the kiss, and it makes tingles rush through my body until it feels like my ovaries are vibrating.

The kiss turns hungry, and soon we're panting, our tongues stroking and lips kneading.

Sigh… I've wanted this for so long.

I take hold of Ryker's shirt and start to tug it up. Letting out a frustrated groan, I mumble, "Take it off."

Ryker grabs hold of the shirt behind his neck and yanks it off.

"Daaayyumm… that was hot," I whisper. My eyes drop to his abs and then lower. I let out a moan. "God, those fuck me muscles are a turn-on."

Ryker wraps an arm around me as his mouth claims mine again. His body presses against mine, and feeling how hard he is against my stomach weakens my legs.

Holy shit, I want this. More than anything.

Ryker's hands drop to my bottom, and when he lifts me against his rock-hard body, I wrap my legs around his waist. He somehow manages to maneuver us to the bed, and then his mouth burns down my neck while his hands settle on my hips. His grip tightens on me before his right hand moves up. With his lips and tongue lashing at my racing pulse, Ryker moves his right hand up until his palm takes the weight of my breast.

God, having his hands on me… it's more intense than I thought it would be.

Needing to touch him as well, I brush my palms down his muscled back. Feeling his body ripple as he begins to tug at my shirt makes my abdomen tighten. Ryker pulls my shirt off, and then his mouth crashes against mine. The kiss is overwhelmingly wild, filled with years of desire and love.

I move a hand between us, my fingers trailing down his chest and abs until I reach the snap of jeans. I manage to get it undone.

Ryker pushes his left hand under my neck while his right hand brushes down the length of my body until his palm slips between my legs.

Intense tingles rush over me when he begins to rub me through my jeans. Needing to feel his skin on me, I try to push his jeans down while whispering, "I need you."

Ryker pulls away from me, and I lift my hips as he undoes my jeans and then yanks them down my legs, along with my panties. While I unsnap my bra, Ryker steps out of his own jeans and boxers.

Before I can drink in the sight of his body, he crawls over me, pressing kisses on my inner thigh.

I let out a throaty moan. "So good. Damn... so... good."

It feels as if he's worshiping me as his tongue lashes at my sensitive skin, and I feel his breath fan over my clit. His tongue swipes over me, and I grab hold of the covers as another moan drifts over my lips.

He begins to alternate between his tongue and teeth, working me into a mindless frenzy, and then my body tightens. When he sucks on my sensitive flesh while pushing a finger inside me, I begin to make sounds roughly resembling a prayer as an intense orgasm robs me of my ability to breathe.

Ryker crawls back up my body, again pressing kisses to my flushed skin. His mouth finds my breast, and his teeth tug on my pebbled bud, sending a spark zapping to my tingling core. It has need slowly building in my abdomen again.

Our movements turn tender, our hands exploring each other. I savor the feel of Ryker's muscles beneath his tanned skin as my palms rub over his back and ass.

Opening my legs wider, Ryker's lower half settles between them, and feeling his cock pressing against me has a breath catching in my throat.

This is a dream come true.

Ryker's eyes lock on mine as he positions himself at my entrance. There's a wave of emotion in my chest as he pushes inside me with one long thrust. My body arches from how full and amazing it feels. My breasts press against his chest, and the mind-blowing feelings draw a moan from me while my fingers dig into his ass.

"Finally," I whisper, my eyes drinking in the sight of him above me. I bring my arms up and wrap them tightly around his neck. Lifting my head, our mouths connect in a hungry kiss as he begins to move, thrusting deep inside me.

"You feel so good," I whisper breathlessly against his lips. "God, harder."

Ryker's whole body moves against mine, our skin memorizing the feel of each other.

"Fuck, Danny," he groans. "You're so fucking wet for me."

"Having you inside me," I gasp, my abdomen starting to tighten, "is heaven."

Ryker grabs hold of my hip, and then he drives into me, deliciously hard and fast.

"Ryker," I moan, so... so... so close to my orgasm as the sound of our pelvises crashing against each other fills the room.

His hand moves in between us, and he begins to rub my clit. It feels as if my body comes apart, splintering with pleasure. I make sounds I'm pretty sure I've never made before.

His body jerks against mine. "I love you, Danny. So fucking much."

My eyes focus on Ryker's face, and I watch as his features tighten while he empties himself inside me. He's never looked hotter than he does at this moment. His jaw clenched, his eyes dark with pleasure, his bottom lip captured between his teeth.

Holy shit, he looks like a sex god.

Then his expression softens with something akin to awe, and it has me lifting my hand to his jaw while I whisper, "I love you too."

Ryker's body stills, and keeping himself buried deep inside me, he lowers his head and kisses me until I begin to feel sleepy.

At some point, he pulls out of me only to slump half over me, and then we drift off.

RYKER

Waking up, there's one hell of bright light shining into the room. I squint, and not recognizing any of the furniture, I lift my hand to my pounding head.

My other senses begin to kick in, and feeling a woman's naked body against me, my eyes snap open again. Glancing down, my lips part as I take in Danny lying half over me. Naked.

Holy. Fuck.

She begins to stir, and every muscle in my body freezes. I can't help but take in the feel of her breasts against my skin and her pussy pressed against my hip.

It's a sensory overload that has me turning hard as steel in a split-second.

Lifting her head, Danny blinks a couple of times, and then her eyes lock on mine. I watch as shock ripples over her face, and then she shoots up onto her knees, giving me one hell of a view of her hot as fuck body.

God, her breasts.

A memory of drawing her nipple into my mouth flashes through my mind. The taste of her pussy. Burying my cock deep inside her. How wet she was for me. Making her orgasm… twice.

Heat spreads through me like a wildfire, but before my eyes can focus on any other part of her body, she covers her mouth and whispers, "Nooooo…. I fucked up."

Her eyes begin to lower to my chest, then to my abs, before they snap back to my face. Just as well. I don't think she can handle the view of my hard cock right now.

Clearing my throat, I say, "Don't panic."

True Danny style, she starts to panic, jumping off the bed and running to the bathroom. I get a look at her perfect ass and then the door slams shut behind her. "Oh God. Oh God. Oh God." There's a moment of silence, then she starts up again. "Oh God. Oh God."

Getting up from the bed, my head spins a little. I walk to the door. "Stop panicking."

"How can I not panic?" she shrieks.

"We had too much to drink, and we had sex. Let's talk about it," I mutter. Staring at the shut door, I start to remember more of the night.

Every beautiful inch of her body.

Thrusting inside her.

I close my eyes, remembering how good it felt.

'I love you too.'

My eyes snap back open as my heart begins to speed up.

She doesn't see me as her little brother's best friend. Fuck, she feels the same about me. Last night is a clear indication of that.

Hope explodes through me.

I can finally be with the woman I love.

Walking back to the bed, I grab my boxers and drag them on. Picking up Danny's clothes, I smile when I see the black boyshorts and a white bra. It's so typical of her.

I walk back to the bathroom and knock. "I have your clothes."

She opens the door, just enough to stick her hand through, and it draws a chuckle from me.

"Stop laughing. This is far from funny," she snaps.

When she shuts the door again, I put on the rest of my clothes. Finding my shirt in the living room, I pull it on, then walk to the kitchen. Putting water in the coffee pot, I wait for it to boil.

When I'm done making coffee, I carry the cups to the bedroom then sit down on the bed. "I have coffee."

The door opens, and Danny comes out looking as bad as I feel.

She takes a mug and sits down next to me. "Thanks."

An awkward silence fills the room as we sip on the coffee.

When Danny's done, she clears her throat. "Do you remember anything?"

Every. Single. Hot as fuck. Moment.

Her question has me frowning. "Yeah... you?"

She sits still for a couple of minutes, then says, "Not much."

"What do you mean by not much?"

She shrugs. "Actually, very little."

74

I stare at her.

Well, that sucks. I have sex with the woman I love, and she can't remember shit.

"We should forget it happened," she mutters.

"You already did," I remind her dryly.

"I mean that we had… you know." She gets up, refusing to look at me.

"Danny." She starts walking to the door, and it has me standing up. "Daniele!" She stops but doesn't turn around. "That's it? We had sex, and you're going to ignore it?"

Finally, she turns around to look at me. "It is what it is. We were drunk. I'm sorry. Being older, I shouldn't have… done what I did."

"What the actual fuck?" I snap at her. It takes me a moment to process what she's saying. "It is what it is?"

I don't get angry quickly, but this is pushing me into the red real fast.

She looks downright miserable. "I'm sorry it happened. I wish I could turn back time and fix this mess. I'm sorry, Ryker."

God, now's the time to give me strength.

Tilting my head, I struggle to keep my composure. "You're sorry? We had sex, and you're sorry? Thanks for the fucking confidence boost."

Her eyes widen, and she takes two steps closer to me before stopping. "I didn't mean it like that. You were great."

"I thought you didn't remember," I bite the words out. Before she can say anything else, I walk by her and out of the room. "We should get going. I have to work on the contract."

Chapter 7

DANNY

Holy shit.

I fucked up.

So… so… so badly.

The drive back to the hotel is painful. I have a headache from hell, and the awkward silence is suffocating. The anger coming off Ryker makes it hard to breathe.

Pressing my lips together, I stare at the nature wooshing past the car.

Oh, Danny. What did you do?

I lied. I remember everything. It was mind-blowingly amazing.

I take a deep breath and let it out slowly.

I might've been drunk, but I remember what it felt like to have Ryker inside me. He was intoxicated, and in the heat of the moment, he probably didn't mean it. But hearing him say 'I love you' had my heart bursting with happiness.

Now it's just a shriveled mess.

Closing my eyes, I let the memories from last night flash through my mind. How hot he looked. His muscled body. Having his hands and mouth on me.

Dear God.

I shift in my seat as desire tightens my abdomen.

Ryker puts on the radio and turns up the volume.

Minutes later, *Kiss Me* begins to play, and my eyes widen.

You. Have. Got. To. Be. Kidding. Me.

He doesn't turn off the radio but instead puts it even louder.

Feeling like shit warmed up, I rest my elbow on the door, and covering my mouth with my hand, I keep my eyes locked on the blur of green flashing by the car.

The song's words take on a whole new meaning, and I close my eyes against the truth.

What I feel for him won't just go away.

I love Ryker.

After last night… I shake my head. We can never be more than friends. I'm almost seven years older than him.

When the song ends, I let out a sigh of relief.

We don't say a word, and by the time we get back to the hotel, it feels like my head's going to split open. Hangover's suck.

Walking into the suite, my head spins, and I only make it to the living room when my legs suddenly give way beneath me, and I drop to the floor with a dull thud.

"Danny!"

Everything goes black.

Seconds later, the pain in my head floods back like a tsunami, and I let out a groan.

"Danny." Ryker's voice is filled with worry, and it's only then I feel his arms around me.

I pry my eyes open and squint against the bright light. "I'm... okay," I manage to slur.

I begin to sit up, and Ryker helps me. Taking a deep breath, I lift my hand to my forehead.

"Headache? Again?" Ryker asks.

"Hangover... from hell," I mutter.

I climb to my feet, and Ryker instantly places an arm around my waist.

"I'm going... to sleep... it off," I mumble. I frown when my sentence comes out weird, as if I'm having difficulty finding the right words to say.

I'm never drinking again.

"I think you should see a doctor," Ryker says.

"For a… hangover?" I chuckle. "I'm fine." I begin to walk to my room, my legs feeling shaky. Reaching the door, I glance at Ryker. "I'm really sorry… about last night… and this morning."

He stares at me for a moment. "We can talk once we both feel less dead."

The corner of my mouth twitches, and then I close the door behind me.

Stripping out of the clothes, I take a bath before putting on a pair of shorts and a t-shirt. Crawling into bed, I let out a groan, and seconds later, I'm fast asleep.

RYKER

It's already late afternoon, and when there's still no sign of Danny, I walk to her room. I knock on the door and wait a moment before pushing it open.

She's still fast asleep, and I consider leaving her, but after she passed out this morning, I've been worried.

I move closer to the bed and sit down on the side. Danny looks fucking hot in the tight shorts and t-shirt, her ass making my hands itch with the need to touch her.

Instead of groping her, I place my hand on her hip and shake her lightly. "Danny."

She begins to wake up and then stretches, the shirt pulling tight over her breasts and showing me the outline of her nipples.

Christ. She looks like a wet dream.

"I didn't want to wake you, but it's already four o'clock. You should eat something," I explain. When her eyes focus on my face, I ask, "How do you feel?"

She sits up and rubs a hand over her face. "Much better. Sorry I slept so long."

"It's okay."

She climbs off the bed and walks to the bathroom. Figuring the rest she had did the trick, and that she feels better, I walk back to the living room and sit down on the couch.

I'm working through the contract's clauses when Danny comes out, wearing a pair of black slacks and a white sweater.

"What do you want to eat?" I ask as she sits down next to me.

"Something solid. Steak or chicken?" She reaches for the financials.

Getting up, I walk to the phone and place our order before heading back to the couch. On purpose, I sit down close to her, my leg pressing against hers.

Danny freezes but doesn't say anything.

After a couple of minutes of just staring at the document, I ask, "Are we going to talk about what happened?"

I hear her take a deep breath. "I don't know what else to say. I'm sorry it happened."

Clenching my jaw, I drop the document on the coffee table and rest my forearms on my thighs. Closing my eyes, I rein in the burst of anger. "Do you regret us having sex?"

I feel her eyes snap to me. "Ahh…"

Turning my gaze to hers, our eyes lock. "Do you regret it, Danny?"

"You're twenty-five," she begins to ramble. "I'm thirty-two."

"I'm well aware of the age gap, and I don't give a shit about it," I grumble.

She shakes her head. "People will talk. The last thing I want is everyone thinking I'm some cougar who took advantage of a younger guy."

"Seriously?" I hiss. "The age gap isn't that much, and I don't care what other people think."

"Ryker," she murmurs, a pleading tone to her voice.

"Do you regret having sex with me?" I ask again.

Her eyes move to the table, and a minute later, she shakes her head. "But it doesn't matter."

"How can you say that?" I ask, my voice dropping low with frustration.

"We work together," she throws a pathetic-ass excuse my way.

"So?"

"Our families will freak out," she keeps going. "Especially Tristan."

"I don't think our families will care," I disagree. "And I'll handle Tristan."

"You're so much younger than me," she returns to the topic of the fucking age gap.

Turning so my body's facing hers, I take hold of her arm. "Look at me."

It takes a couple of seconds before Danny's gaze meets mine.

"We made love. It was fucking amazing. I don't regret a single moment." She begins to shake her head, and needing to get through to her makes me go in for the kill. "I love you, and I'm pretty sure you said those same words to me while I was buried deep inside of you."

Danny covers her face with her hands, letting out a groan. "We were drunk," she exclaims.

Letting out a frustrated groan, I say, "I'm not drunk right now. Did you not hear what I just said, or are you choosing to ignore it?"

Danny's lips part, but before she can say something, the doorbell rings. I let out a sigh as I get up to open the door. A server pushes a cart into the suite, and after I've signed for it, he leaves. Picking up the two plates, I carry them to the dining table.

Aggravated out of my mind, I place my hands on the glass surface of the table and close my eyes.

I hear Danny move, and then she says, "I'm going for a walk. I think we both need some space to think."

I dart toward her and grab hold of her arm before she can even open the door. "You're not going out there alone. It's not safe." I drag her back to the dining room. "And you need to eat."

Danny lets out a huff, but she doesn't argue and takes a seat.

I have zero appetite, but I sit down and begin to cut into the steak while grumbling, "Eat, Daniele."

She shoots me a glare. "That's the second time today you've called me by my full name."

"Because you fucking listen then," I mutter as I get up to grab two bottles of water from the fridge.

I set one down in front of her, and uncapping mine, I take a sip. I stare at the food, which looks amazing, but I can't bring myself to take a bite. Neither can Danny, by the looks of it.

Letting out a sigh, I look at her. "I love you, Danny."

This time she can't ignore the words. She closes her eyes and takes a quivering breath, which has me reaching over and wrapping my fingers around the back of her neck.

"I. Love. You," I say again. "So fucking much it's driving me insane."

Chapter 8

DANNY

Hearing the words, again and again, makes tears blur my vision.

I get up and put some distance between Ryker and me.

I love him and knowing he feels the same makes it impossible to force the words over my lips. I can't deny the one thing I want most in the world.

Ryker West. My happily ever after.

When I shake my head, he closes the distance between us. Taking hold of my shoulders, he leans down to catch my eyes. "Tell me you don't love me, and I'll back off."

I shake my head again as my chin begins to quiver. I can't say those words to him. Never.

Ryker presses his forehead to mine, a pleading tone making his voice hoarse as he whispers, "Please, Danny. Please give us a chance."

Feeling his breath so near my lips has me lifting my hands to his waist. A tear spirals over my cheek, and then I press my mouth to his.

This time there's no alcohol to blame. We both know what we're doing. Ryker's arms wrap around me and tilting his head, his lips nip at mine.

I move my hands to his jaw, and when our tongues touch, I have to lean into him from how intense it feels.

Ryker doesn't deepen the kiss but instead pulls a little back. His eyes jump over my face. "I want you, Danny. God, I want you." I let out a sob, and it has him saying, "It's okay that you want me too. We're both adults. This choice is only for us to make."

He's right.

All I've ever wanted was someone to call my own. A man I can love and build a life with.

Never in my wildest dreams did I think that man would be Ryker West.

But he's the one I want. My prince.

When I nod, Ryker takes a step back from me, surprise tightening his features.

"I need to hear you say it, Danny," he whispers, his voice tense.

"I want you too." A weird sound escapes me, something between a sob and a chuckle. "I can't say no to the one thing I want most in this world."

Emotion washes over Ryker's face, and then his body slams into mine. His arms clamp me to his chest as he buries his face in my hair. "God, Danny. God,' he sighs, the relief heavy in his voice.

I wrap my arms around his waist as happiness unfurls in my chest, and then I admit, "It's been so hard ignoring how I feel about you. Especially with you teasing me every chance you got."

His body shakes as he lets out a chuckle. "How long have you felt this way?"

"Since you started at Indie Ink." I scrunch my nose. "Nope, that's a lie. It started the summer break of your senior year."

Ryker moves his hands up, and framing my face, he pulls back so he can stare into my eyes. "Say it."

I take a deep breath as my eyes drift over his handsome face before they lock on his warm gaze. "I love you, Ryker."

His mouth finds mine, and the kiss is filled with so much hunger, all I can do is hold onto him. Then it actually sinks in. Ryker is kissing me. My heart bursts wide open, and a world of dreams begins to weave around him.

His tongue sweeps through my mouth and then strokes against mine with so much confidence it robs me of my breath. His teeth begin to tug at my lips, and soon our desperate breaths fill the air.

By the time he breaks the kiss, I'm gasping, my lips numb with tingles.

Ryker takes two steps back, looking like the sex god I remember from last night. His lips are parted, and he looks like he's a second away from ravishing me. My body floods with desire, stronger than anything I've felt before.

Somehow he reins his desire in, and then we just stare at each other.

Our breathing calm, and the longer our eyes remain locked, the more overwhelming the moment becomes.

It feels surreal.

My tongue darts out, and wetting my lips, I taste Ryker. My voice sounds uneven when I ask, "What now?"

"I'm just taking in this moment," he murmurs. After a short while, the corner of his mouth curves up. "We're doing this."

"Doing what?" I ask. A dull ache starts in the back of my head.

Now's not the time to get a headache.

"Dating," Ryker replies. "A relationship. Whatever you want to call it." He lets out a chuckle, his lips curving more.

"Dating," I test the word. Us. In a relationship. Worry creeps into my mind. "What if things don't work out between us?"

"I know what I want, Danny, and it's you. I'm not going to change my mind," he states, sounding sure of himself.

"What if our feelings change later on?"

He lets out a breath as he shakes his head. "After eleven years, that's not going to happen. At least not from my side."

"What do you mean eleven years?" I frown at him.

"At first, there was the teenage crush, and then I fell in love. One way or another, it's always been you," he admits.

Wow.

Ryker walks back to me, and lifting his hands, he places them on the sides of my neck.

His touch… God, feeling his hands on me is enough to make me throw caution to the wind.

I take a deep breath then say, "I guess we're doing this."

The sinful smirk tugs at his lips, and it has me pushing up on my toes and pressing a kiss to his mouth, and then I whisper, "That smirk is what had me falling head over heels for you."

"Yeah?" he murmurs, wrapping an arm around me.

"Yeah." A smile spreads over my face, but then it fades again. "What are we going to do when we get home?"

He shakes his head. "Leave that to me. Okay? Don't get stuck in your head about it."

"Easier said than done," I mutter.

Ryker presses a soft kiss to my lips, then whispers, "Trust me, Danny. I'll take care of everything."

RYKER

After we've eaten, we get settled on the couch. Opening my laptop, I bring up my emails.

For a moment, I just stare at the screen.

Fuck, this is really happening. Danny's mine. She's finally mine.

A wave of happiness almost robs me of my breath. Leaning back against the couch, I turn my head and let my eyes drift over Danny. Unable to stop myself, I lift a hand to the back of her neck and brush my thumb over her skin.

God, I'm allowed to touch her, and it feels incredible.

Danny glances at me, her mouth curving up into a sexy smile before she looks at the spreadsheet on her laptop.

I'm grateful we still have two weeks in Cape Town. She'll be used to being in a relationship with me by the time we have to leave.

God, this is really happening.

A smile spreads over my face, and just because I can, I move my hands to the sides of her face and turn her to me. Leaning in, I press a tender kiss to her mouth.

Danny grins against my lips. "Work, Ryker."

"Yes, ma'am," I murmur, and it makes her smile widen.

Focusing on my emails, I see there are a couple from Mr. Cutler at CRC Holdings. We help each other out with the two companies, and once he retires, Noah, my cousin, will be taking over Mr. Cutler's side of things.

It takes me a while to answer every email, and when I finally sit back, I let out a groan.

Danny glances up from her laptop. "Tired?"

"Just stiff."

She lets out a burst of laughter. "How do you do that? Make simple things sound so sexual?"

A grin forms around my lips, and locking eyes with her, I murmur, "It's 'cause you want me." I reach over, and picking up her laptop, I place it on the table.

Danny watches me. "What are you doing? We need to work."

"Break time," I say, and leaning a little forward, I bring my hand to her face and trail my fingers over her cheek and jaw. "God, your skin is so soft."

She leans into my touch, a smile curving her lips.

I begin to move closer but stop when my mouth is an inch from hers. I let the anticipation build as my lips brush over her cheek.

Danny turns her face a little, and when I feel her breath on my jaw, my eyes drift shut from how amazing it feels.

I bring my mouth back to hers and only nip at her lips before slightly pulling back. Our eyes lock, and the moment feels loaded.

I drop my hand to her neck, and then I kiss her. I thrust my tongue into her mouth, trying to memorize the feel of her.

Danny lifts her hands to my shoulders, and then they slip behind my neck and into my hair.

The moment is perfect and exactly how I imagined kissing her would be.

When I break the kiss, I pull her against me as I lean back against the couch. My arms tighten around her, and I have to stop myself from squashing her. "It's incredible to hold you… to kiss you. Finally."

Danny rests her cheek against my chest and places her hand on my abs. "It still feels a little surreal."

"Yeah, it does," I agree. I press my mouth to her hair and take a deep breath of her scent. "You smell so good."

She rubs her cheek against me. "So do you." Suddenly she sits upright and grins at me. "Say 'ma'am' again."

A broad smile forms on my face. "I knew you always liked when I called you that," I tease her.

"It's a turn on," she admits.

"I bet it is, ma'am."

Her lips part and her eyes rake hungrily over me. Reaching for her, I pull her onto my lap, so she's straddling me. I stare into her eyes, unable to believe Danny, the woman I've always dreamed of, is mine to touch and love.

Slipping my hand behind her neck, I begin to nip at her mouth, and the kiss quickly turns wild and downright dirty. It has my cock hardening, and the instant Danny feels it, she starts to rub herself against me. Her movements are so sensual it robs me of my self-control.

Only then do I think to ask, "Are you on birth control?" She nods, and it has me saying, "Good because I'm pretty sure I didn't use a condom last night."

"God, last night," she groans as she presses herself down on my cock. "I need a repeat."

"Yeah?" I murmur.

Danny nods, her hips swiveling.

I drop my voice low and deep as I ask, "Do you need me to fuck you, Daniele?"

Her lashes lower over her eyes, and desire tightens her features. "Yes."

Wrapping my arm around her lower back, I push up to my feet. Danny clamps her legs around me, and then I walk us to her bedroom.

I carefully lie her down on the mattress, and bracing myself on my hands on either side of her head, I stare down at her.

I wish I could find the words to express how I feel about her, but instead, I lower my mouth to her neck as my hands begin to undress her.

Danny manages to get my clothes off, and then she scoots up to the middle of the bed. I crawl over her as my eyes feast on her body. "God, Danny. You're a damn masterpiece."

Lowering my head, my lips and tongue take turns tasting her skin as I start at her neck and work my way down to her body. I take my time exploring every inch of her.

When her fingers wrap around my cock, I pump into her hold a couple of times before I kneel between her legs. Taking hold of her hips, I tug her against me, so her legs are forced to open wide.

My eyes lower to her pussy, and the sight of her in such a vulnerable position makes protectiveness rear inside me.

She really trusts me.

The thought is overpowering.

I take hold of my cock and rub the head over her clit. Danny looks scorching hot as she grabs hold of the covers while letting out a seductive as fuck moan.

Glancing down, I watch as I rub myself against her until her breaths begin to speed up. "Ryker...please!"

Smirking, I lean forward, and bracing my forearms on either side of her head, I stare into her eyes. "Please?"

"Oh God, just fuck me already. I'm about to spontaneously combust."

I move my right hand down the side of her body. "Tell me what you like, Daniele. What makes you come."

"Your mouth and cock," she groans, arching her body to rub her breasts against my chest.

"How do you make yourself come?" I ask, knowing I'm torturing her and loving every second.

"Again, your mouth and cock, just in my imagination," she grumbles, clearly frustrated.

Rocking forward, I slide my cock through her slick heat, and it draws another moan from her. I drop my voice lower. "Yeah? You fantasized about me? In the office? In your bed?"

"Everywhere," she gasps and wrapping her arms around me, her hands find my ass, and her fingers dig in.

I position myself at her entrance, and then our eyes lock. "This is me claiming you," I growl as I push inside her. Feeling her inner muscles wrap around me makes my body shudder with pleasure. I pull out and thrust hard inside her. "This is me promising I'll never let you go."

Danny lifts her head, and then her lips and tongue work me into a wild mess. My hips follow the movement of her tongue, and there's so much pleasure, I feel drunk all over again.

Drunk on love. Who knew it was an actual thing?

Chapter 9

DANNY

I'm sad our business trip is coming to an end. It turned out to be a dream come true instead of torture.

Ryker tightens his hold on my hand as he pulls me out of the cable car. We walk to a lookout point on top of Table Mountain and stare at the Atlantic Ocean.

I lean my cheek against his bicep. "I don't want to go home. Let's run away and stay here."

He lets out a chuckle. "Okay."

"Such a bad influence," I tease him.

"Yeah, look what's become of you," he chuckles.

I glance up at him, "What's become of me?"

"I turned you into an addict who can't get enough of my cock."

Slapping his arm, I glance around to see if anyone else heard what he said. Seeing it's safe, I scowl up at him, but before I can say anything, his mouth crashes against mine.

It feels like I'm standing on top of the world as I wrap my arms around his neck.

When he pulls back, he murmurs, "I love you so much."

I let out a happy sigh, which turns into a shriek when he lifts me off my feet, spinning us in a circle. Letting go of him, I throw my arms wide and tilt my head up to the sun while laughter bubbles over my lips.

The past three weeks, I've known more happiness than in my entire life combined. And I've had a happy life, so that's saying a lot.

When Ryker lowers me, my hands find his jaw, and I press a tender kiss to his mouth. "Who would've thought I'd come here to conquer the continent, and instead, I managed to get you as well."

Ryker takes hold of my hand, and linking our fingers, we begin to follow a trail. Everywhere I look, there are wildflowers.

My happy smile tightens as a sharp pain shoots through my head, and then my vision fades to black. My steps falter, and my legs lose all feeling. Before I can hit the ground, Ryker grabs hold of me. "Danny?"

"Just... dizzy," I mumble, my speech slurring.

As my vision begins to return, Ryker carefully lowers me to the ground and crouches behind me so I can lean against him.

"Probably… from… the… spinning," I say, my voice halting between words as if I'm struggling to remember how to form a sentence.

"I'm sorry," he murmurs, brushing the hair from my face. "Feeling better?"

I close my eyes and take a couple of deep breaths. "Yeah."

He helps me up and wraps his arm around me, pulling me to his side. I hold onto him, my legs still feel shaky.

"Do you want to go back?" Ryker asks.

I shake my head and point to a bench. "Can we… sit?"

"Sure." Ryker keeps our pace slow, and once I'm seated on the bench, I focus on taking deep breaths. The sharp pain has reduced to a dull ache.

Another damn headache?

It's happening more and more. Not jumping to conclusions, I decide to visit a doctor once we're back in the states. It's probably just stress from signing the new deal.

I lean into Ryker, resting my head against his chest.

"Better?" he asks before pressing a kiss to my hair.

"Perfect," I whisper.

When I glance up at him, he presses a kiss to my mouth. "Are you sure it's from the spinning?"

Hearing the concern in his voice, I smile widely. "I'm sure. I guess you just have a way… of sweeping my feet from under me."

My words make him smile, and he seems to relax.

I begin to feel nauseous, and it has my eyebrow popping up.

Shit. What if I'm pregnant? Birth control isn't foolproof.

RYKER

Rubbing my hand up and down Danny's arm, I feel when she tenses, and it has my eyes sharpening on her. "What's wrong?"

She shakes her head as she sits up, then she says, "I feel nauseous."

"Do you think it's something you ate?" I ask, my worry coming back in full force.

Again, she shakes her head.

I tilt my head, and the corner of my mouth tugs up. "You're dizzy and nauseous. Do you think…"

Danny lets out a chuckle, then she mutters, "It would be… just my luck. I'll do a test… when we get home."

My smile keeps growing. "What if you're pregnant?"

She begins to laugh. "One step at a time."

"But what if?" I push.

"Well…then I suppose… we're having a baby," she says, shaking her head.

"How do you feel about having kids with me?" I ask directly.

"I've always wanted kids. I was just hoping… to take things… a hell of a lot slower."

It's my turn to chuckle. "I'm not going anywhere," I say just in case she's worried about that. "I'm in for the long haul."

Danny leans forward, resting her chin on her hand and her elbow on her knee, then her ocean-blue gaze finds mine. "Yeah? You want to be… my baby-daddy?"

Leaning forward, I press a kiss to her lips, then murmur, "It would be a dream come true."

"How many kids… do you want?" she asks.

My eyes sharpen on her again when the way she's talking grabs my attention. There are pauses between her words, but she doesn't seem to notice.

"Two to three would be great," I reply.

A breeze begins to play with her brown strands, pushing some across her face. I reach for her, tucking the strands behind her ear.

"And you? How many do you want?" I ask, love for her filling every inch of my heart and pushing the worry back because she looks fine.

"The same." Danny turns her gaze to the ocean and takes a deep breath. "I had it all... planned out. My life. I'd meet the man... of my dreams... at twenty-eight. We'd get married at thirty, and we'd have our... first child at thirty-two."

I lift my hand again, brushing my fingers over her cheek as I move her hair behind her ear.

Her mouth curves up as her eyes find mine again. "Wouldn't it be funny... if it all happened now?"

"Why would it be funny?" I ask.

She shrugs, then whispers, "You're only twenty-five."

"So?"

"Aren't there things... you want to do before settling down?" Danny asks.

I shake my head. "I'm happy with my career. I have my own place. I've traveled. The only thing missing from my life was you."

Danny's smile softens. "It's crazy... how much has changed... during this trip."

"Yeah, I just needed to get you alone," I joke.

"Oh, so you planned this?" she asks, her eyebrow raising.

"No, but I sure as fuck hoped for it." We stare at each other in silence, and after a couple of minutes, I ask, "Tell me about your dreams."

"I just did," she chuckles.

"Is there nothing you still want to do? A bucket list of sorts? Where do you want to raise our kids? In the city or suburbs?"

Danny leans over and kisses me tenderly, then she whispers against my lips, "Our kids?"

"Yeah," I murmur.

We pull apart and go back to staring at each other. "I'd like a house in the suburbs. You know... the white picket fence dream."

"I'd like that as well," I admit. "A basketball hoop, up above the garage. A swing on the porch."

"Lots of flowers in the garden," she murmurs.

When she's quiet again, I ask, "What else?"

"I don't want a traditional wedding."

"Yeah? No white dress, church, huge-ass reception?"

She chuckles. "No." Danny's eyes drift over the nature around us. "I always pictured a field... with wildflowers and just relaxing... with my family and friends afterward."

"Sounds right up my alley."

Danny turns her gaze to me, and emotion makes them shimmer like sapphires. "It's been two weeks... and it's still surreal."

"That we're together?" I ask as I reach for her hand, linking my fingers with hers.

"Yeah," she whispers. Her tongue darts out, and she wets her lips. "Can we keep it between us... for a while? I just need to get used to us... before telling everyone."

If it were up to me, I'd be shouting off the top of this mountain, but respecting Danny's wish, I agree, "Okay."

"So, no shenanigans at the office," she warns me.

"Damn, there goes hot office sex on your desk," I tease her.

My comment draws laughter from her, and pulling her to my chest, I wrap my arms around her. With my mouth pressed to her hair, I stare at the dark blue ocean.

I came to South Africa thinking a relationship between us will never happen. Tomorrow we're leaving as a couple.

I'll never forget this trip.

It changed my entire life.

"Love you," I whisper against her hair.

"Love you too."

Chapter 10

DANNY

Being back in the states, I feel nervous about Ryker and me. I'm worried now that we're home, things will change. Like the relationship was only a part of our trip, and it's time to return to reality.

My phone pings, and picking it up, I see there's a text from Ryker.

R: Can we have dinner tonight?

My worry grows. What if he wants to break things off? Shit.

D: Where do you want to meet?

My heartbeat speeds up while I wait for his reply.

R: I'll be at your place at seven.

I take a deep breath as I stare at the words.

Don't jump to conclusions, Danny.

It's just… I'm terrified of losing Ryker, and I hate not being in control.

Letting out a sigh, I check the time and seeing it's already past five o'clock, I decide to get ready.

After showering and washing my hair, I dry it before pulling a straightener through the strands. I take care applying my make-up, wanting to look my best.

When I'm done, I check my reflection in the mirror. I've gone with black pants and a light blue cashmere sweater seeing as it's still chilly outside.

Relax, Danny.

Just relax.

Deep breaths.

When my phone begins to ring, I startle, then go to answer it.

Seeing it's the concierge, I answer, "Yes?"

"There's a Mr. West to see you, ma'am."

"Send him up."

I end the call then take a couple of deep breaths. Picking up my clutch, I tuck the phone inside, and then I walk to the living room. My eyes are glued to the elevator, and when the doors slide open, my heart explodes into a wild beat.

Ryker looks hot as hell in his brown chinos and a black button-up shirt. The fabric does nothing to hide his muscles.

As he walks toward me, a frown appears between his eyes, and tilting his head, he asks, "Why do you look nervous."

Yeah, my acting skills have gone to hell.

Swallowing hard, I say, "Just a little nervous now that we're home."

His mouth curves up, and stopping in front of me, he leans down and presses a tender kiss to my lips. He pulls a little back, his eyes drifting over my face. "Is that all it is?"

I begin to nod but then admit, "I'm not sure what it means for us."

Again, he tilts his head, his gaze locking with mine. "Are you having second thoughts?"

Quickly, I shake my head. "No, not at all. I just wasn't sure you wanted to continue dating or whether it was a case of what happened in Africa stays in Africa."

Ryker takes a step back, a frown tightening his features. "Did I give you the impression I wasn't serious?"

"No," I whisper, then I shrug. "It's… uhm… you're." I let out a breath. "It's still surreal."

Understanding flashes over his face, and then he pulls me against his chest, his arms wrapping tightly around me. "I'm not having second thoughts. I meant every word I said. You're it for me, Danny, and nothing will change that. Okay?"

I nod as I bring my hands up to his shoulders. "I'm sorry. I don't like not being in control." I glance up at him. "It's making me psycho."

Ryker brings his hands up to the sides of my neck. "Why do you feel like you don't have control?"

"I'm just not good at the dating thing," I chuckle. "One of the reasons I'm still single at thirty-two."

"The other reasons?" he asks.

A smile tugs at my lips. "You."

Ryker gives me a quick kiss, then he murmurs, "You know me, Danny. I'm not going to change just because we're dating."

Also true.

Ryker's eyes meet mine again. "I think we should stay in and talk. I don't like you feeling unsure about us."

Nodding, I gesture to the couch. "Can I get you something to drink?"

Ryker shakes his head, and taking hold of my hand, he pulls me to the couch. When we sit down, I place my clutch on the coffee table.

"Tell me everything you're worried about," he says as he turns his body toward mine.

Relaxing into the cushion, I say, "My brothers. I'm not so worried about Christopher, but Tristan's going to lose his mind.

"When you're ready, I'll tell him. He'll understand," Ryker tries to reassure me.

Giving him a look, I say, "He beat the last guy I dated."

"Because that guy was an asshole," Ryker mutters.

My eyebrow darts up. "What makes you say that?"

Ryker's eyes lock on mine, then he asks, "You knew he was abusive, right? Tristan found out, and that's why he beat him up."

Surprise ripples through me. "I didn't know that."

Ryker tilts his head. "Don't worry about Tristan and me. He'll be glad you're with someone who will treat you right."

My lips curve up. "Yeah, I didn't think of it that way."

"Anything else you're worried about?"

"Just that people will think it's weird. You know, with me being older," I admit.

Ryker lets out a breath of air, and then he lifts his hand to the side of my neck. His thumb brushes over my skin, making me lean into his touch. "Are you happy with us dating?"

"Of course."

He shakes his head lightly. "Then what does it matter what people think?"

"I just don't want people laughing behind my back," I mutter.

"If you're referring to the staff, they wouldn't dare. Those who don't respect you fear you."

I pull a disgruntled face. "You make it sound like I'm a tyrant."

"No, only the person who pays their salaries."

My gaze drifts over Ryker's features, and seeing how sincere he is, it washes the last of my reservations away. "Thanks for listening. I know I'm overdramatic, but…" I wet my lips, then admit, "I don't want to lose you."

A smile curves his mouth, and then he leans in, pressing a kiss to my lips. "You won't." He pulls a little back. "Just in case you don't know, I'm fucking crazy about you, Danny. This… us being in a relationship… it's everything I've ever wanted."

This time I lean into him, and I let my mouth brush over his jaw. "I'm crazy about you too."

———————————

RYKER

Being back at work, there's a lot to catch up with. I've just finalized the contract for Take3, and walking into Danny's office, I grin when I see her scowling at her screen.

"Who's in trouble?" I ask as I drop the folder on her desk.

She glances at me, and the tension instantly fades. "Oh, no one. Is this the Take3 contract?"

"Yeah. It just needs everyone's signatures." I walk around her desk, and placing my hand on the back of her chair, I turn her toward me. Danny tilts her head back to look at me as I bring my other hand to her jaw. Leaning down, I steal a kiss. "I really want to fuck you on your desk," I murmur against her lips.

Danny lets out a chuckle as she shakes her head. "Get back to work."

"Slave driver and a cock block," I grumble playfully before I kiss her again.

I've just straightened up when her door opens, and Christopher comes in. Danny instantly looks worried, and it has me reaching for the folder. "Hey, you're just in time to sign." I take out the document and then lean closer to

Danny while I point out everywhere her signature is needed.

She gives me a grateful smile.

I turn my gaze to Christopher as he takes a seat across from Danny. "Three more weeks until the wedding. Are you excited?"

"Yeah, I can't wait." He grins at me, and then he begins to sign the pages Danny's pushing his way.

When they're both done, I gather all the pages and place them in order. I double-check that they didn't miss anything. "I'll get the others to sign, then bring it back," I tell Danny as I place the contract back in the folder.

"Thanks, Ryker," Danny says as I walk away from her desk. Before I pull the door shut behind me, I wink at her, and it makes her smile.

I stop by Dash's desk, and once she's signed, I take the elevator down to my floor.

When I walk into Noah's office, he and Kao are giving each other a brotherly hug. They both have huge grins on their faces.

"What did I miss?" I ask.

Kao's smile widens, then he says, "Fallon's pregnant."

Wrapping my arm around Kao's shoulders, I say, "That's great news. Congrats."

I hold the folder out to him. "I need you and Noah to sign."

Kao takes a seat at Noah's desk, and I wait while they read over the document and sign wherever I've marked.

When I'm done, I send Uncle Rhett a text asking him to stop by the office. He's still signing everything until his daughter, Jade, graduates from college this coming May.

As soon as I'm back in my office, I pull my phone out and send Danny a text.

R: Have I told you it's a turn-on watching you run this company?

It takes a couple of minutes before she replies.

D: You haven't.

D: Be in my office at ten pm, and I'll let you fuck me on my desk.

My lips instantly curve up.

R: How do you expect me to get any work done now?

D: Oops, my bad.

I let out a chuckle. Shaking my head, I have to force myself to not sit and fantasize about Danny naked on her desk.

Fuck, tonight can't come soon enough.

Chapter 11

DANNY

The first week back in the states has been beyond hectic. I don't know if I'm coming or going.

There's so much work to catch up with, but not feeling well, I decide to visit the ER during my lunch hour.

"I'm probably just pregnant," I tell the doctor again.

He smiles at me. "We'll know soon enough, but just in case you're not, we'll run a bunch of tests. Okay?" He begins doing a routine check, then asks, "Besides the headaches, dizzy spells, and nausea, is there anything else?"

"My vision blurs during the dizzy spells, and my legs go numb. There are also times where… it's a struggle to talk like my words are stilted. It's hard to explain."

The nurse who took my urine to do a pregnancy test comes back to say, "The test is negative."

Shoot. I was actually excited about the idea that I might be pregnant.

There's a stab of disappointment in my chest as the doctor shines a light into my eyes. "I'd like to run a CT scan, as well as do some bloodwork. Just so we can eliminate all the possibilities."

"Okay."

I have to fill out a bunch of paperwork and patiently sit while a nurse draws blood. As soon as I have a moment alone, I call Christopher's number.

"Hey, where are you? I just checked your office," my brother answers.

"I'm out running some errands... Then I lost my credit card.... I'm stuck at the bank. Can you cover for me? Please." I feel horrible for lying to Christopher, but I don't want him to worry.

"Of course."

I see the nurse walking back to me and quickly say, "Thanks. I appreciate it. Catch you later."

I cut the call just as the nurse reaches me. "Let's get that CT scan done. You'll need to take off all your jewelry."

I remove the ring on my right hand, then my watch and earrings, and drop them in one of my handbag's side pockets. I also have to change into a hospital gown because my suit has zippers.

The whole procedure takes a while, and lying on the bed as the machine scans over me, my thoughts return to the business trip and how amazing Ryker's been since we've been back.

I still can't believe Ryker actually loves me. He's been so attentive and sweet, melting my heart.

How lucky am I?

When the scan is done, I let out a sigh of relief, thinking they're not going to find anything.

I change back into my clothes and take a seat in the designated waiting area. Forty minutes later, I begin to feel edgy, needing to get back to work. My eyes keep darting to my watch, and I wonder if I shouldn't call Christopher again.

Finally, the ER doctor comes toward me. There's a comforting smile on his face, one he probably wears every single day.

"Okay, so we did find something. He turns the scan so I can see, but I have no idea what I'm looking at. "It looks like you have a growth in your right frontal lobe. We'll need to do an MRI, though."

His words don't sink in, and I can only nod. "Okay. Now?"

"Yes, if you don't mind changing back into the hospital gown. A nurse will be with you shortly."

I go through the motions, my mind stunned into a haze. Once I'm wearing the hospital gown, I lift my hand to my mouth as the doctor's words repeat in my mind.

A growth.

In my head.

Oh my God.

Anxiety begins to build in my chest with every passing minute.

The nurse comes to get me and leads me to another room where I have to lie down again, keeping as still as I possibly can.

This time I don't keep myself busy thinking of Ryker, but instead, I keep replaying what the doctor said over and over.

A growth.

In my brain.

That can't be good.

Time warps into a panicky mess, and every couple of minutes, my heart begins to race before calming again.

I don't even know how long I've been at the hospital when I'm done with the MRI and taken to the neurology floor.

My stomach suddenly drops as it starts to sink in. I have a growth in my head.

Oh God. This is bad. Right? Anything in the brain is bad.

My breathing speeds up, and I struggle to keep my shit together when I'm shown to an examination room. I glance around at the desk, the chairs, the freaking blinds, anything to try and keep my mind busy.

A doctor comes in, and the first thing I notice is the intelligence shining from his eyes.

"Hi, I'm Dr. Friedman. I'm a neurosurgeon." After we shake hands, he makes a fist and says, "You have a tumor in your right frontal lobe roughly the size of half my fist. We have to schedule a biopsy so we can get a sample of the tumor to see what kind it is."

"What does that entail?" I ask, my voice sounding calm while everything in me just goes numb.

"You'll be here for two days," he begins to explain, "We'll drill a small hole in your skull and insert a hollow needle into the incision. We'll extract a sample of the tissue so we can send it for testing." As the words keep coming, my mind goes into denial.

It's probably nothing a quick surgery can't fix.

"Is it bad?" I ask.

"We won't know for sure until we've done a biopsy. We'll be able to discuss treatment options then."

Dr. Friedman goes on to ask me about my family history, and it's only then I think to say, "My grandmother died of cancer. I don't know what kind, though. I'll have to check with my mom."

"Find out as much about your grandmother's history as you can. Information is always a good thing to have." He gives me a comforting smile, which only makes me more anxious.

Dr. Friedman schedules the biopsy for two days from now. My mind starts racing, searching for a valid excuse to give my family and friends, why I'll be gone from the office for two days. Seeing as the biopsy is on Friday, I'll only miss a day at work. But still…

God, what am I going to tell Ryker?

Six hours later, I finally leave the hospital and drive back to the office. Knowing most of the staff at Indie Ink are getting ready to go home is a comfort. I just want to get lost in work and not think about the tumor.

Denial is a blissful thing, and right now, I'm trying to embrace it with open arms.

———————————

RYKER

Worried and unable to focus on my work, I try Danny's phone again. Christopher said she was stuck at the bank, but damn, how long can it take to get a credit card?

When the call goes unanswered, I take the elevator up to Danny's office. Her PA, James, is busy packing up when I reach his desk. "Is Danny back?"

He nods. "She just got back ten minutes ago."

"Are you heading home?" I ask as I walk to her door.

"Yes, have a good evening," he smiles as he walks down the hallway.

"You too." Opening the door, I walk inside, and seeing Danny behind her desk, I let out a sigh of relief. I shut the door behind me, then say, "I was worried."

She keeps staring at the file in front of her, not saying anything.

I walk around her desk and crouch next to her chair. A frown forms on my forehead when she doesn't even notice me. "Hey, are you okay?"

Slowly, as if she's in a haze, she turns her head, and then she blinks. "Oh... hey."

"What's wrong?" I ask, my eyes searching her face.

"Nothing." She shakes her head. "Just tired."

"Then go home and get some rest." I rise to my feet.

Danny takes a deep breath, then shakes her head again. "I'll be fine." When I don't move, she asks, "Did you need something?"

Her eyes are on the file in front of her, and for some reason, it bothers me. "Look at me."

"Ryker, I have work to do," she mutters, sounding irritated.

"Daniele, look at me," I say again.

She lets out a sigh then glares up at me. "What? I have work to do. We spoke about this."

Ignoring her words, I ask, "What's wrong?"

"God. Nothing! I just have a lot of work," she snaps, raising her voice at me. "Do you have to be so needy?"

Her outburst sends my temper into the red, and not wanting to get into a fight with her at the office, I walk away.

Stalking down the hallway, Dash comes toward me. "Is Danny in her office?"

"Yeah, and in a piss poor mood. Good luck," I grumble as I pass by Dash.

I slam the button for the elevator, which thankfully opens immediately. I walk inside and press the button for my floor.

Fuck, I can't believe she spoke to me like that.

Stepping out onto my floor, I walk to my office and slam the door shut behind me. When I sit down behind my desk, I take a couple of deep breaths to calm down.

Placing my elbow on the armrest, I rest my chin on my thumb while pressing my forefinger to my mouth. Staring blankly at my laptop screen, I replay what just happened, trying to make sense of it.

The next moment my door opens, and Danny comes in. I don't move a muscle as my eyes lock on her. She shuts the door, and walking to my desk, she takes a seat opposite me.

Her gaze meets mine, and then she says, "I'm sorry I snapped at you. I'm just stressed, but it was no reason to take it out on you."

Lowering my hand, my eyes scan over her face. "I understand you're stressed, but don't ever raise your voice at me."

Danny nods as she slumps back in the chair, looking defeated. It has me asking, "Is it just work?"

She shakes her head but then says, "Yeah. The pressure's just getting to me."

When her chin begins to quiver, I get up from my chair and walk around the desk. Taking hold of her shoulders, I pull her up, and then I wrap my arms around her.

Her body begins to shudder, and hearing a sob, worry floods me. "I get a feeling it's more than work," I murmur, worried she's hiding something from me.

Danny wraps her arms around me, and she sounds fragile when she says, "I'm not pregnant."

God, that explains a lot. She was starting to get excited about the idea and must be disappointed.

Lowering my head, I murmur, "Sorry, babe. If it's that important to you, go off birth control."

She shakes her head. "It's probably for the best. I just got my hopes up. It's stupid. We've only been dating three weeks."

"It's not like I'm some stranger you need to get to know," I mutter, then I add, "I just want to see you happy."

She pulls a little back and uses her fingers to wipe the tears from under her eyes. "I'll be fine."

It doesn't sound like she believes the words.

"What can I do to help lessen the stress?"

The corner of her mouth lifts slightly, and she makes a cute face. "Not be angry with me."

I let out a chuckle. "Done. What else?"

Danny closes her eyes, and it looks like she just realized something terrible.

"Danny?"

She buries her face against my chest, and then she cries like I've never heard her cry before. My arms instantly tighten around her as the worry returns tenfold.

Pressing a hand to the back of her head, I lower my mouth to her ear. "This can't just be stress. Did something happen you're not telling me?"

She shakes her head but doesn't say anything as she grips me for dear life.

I hold her until she calms down, and when she pulls back again, she says, "I think I should go home and sleep. I'm just overtired."

"Is that really all it is?"

Because it feels like a hell of a lot more than just her being tired.

She nods then gives me a pleading look. "Can you take me home?"

"Of course." I grab my phone and keys, then place my arm around her. "Let's go."

"I just need to get my handbag from my office."

I hand her my car key. "I'll get it quickly. Go get in the car."

"Thanks."

We take separate elevators, and once I have Danny's handbag, I head down to the basement.

When we get to Danny's apartment block and I park the car, she asks, "Do you want to come up?"

"Sure."

We take the elevator up, and once inside, I set my keys down on the kitchen counter. Danny does look exhausted, and opening my arms, I say, "Come here, babe."

She doesn't hesitate, and snuggling against my chest, she lets out a heavy sigh.

Leaning down, I murmur, "Why don't you take a relaxing bath while I order dinner?"

She nods and tilts her head back, her eyes finding mine. There's something in her blue irises I can't quite place. Almost as if she's sad.

"You know you can tell me anything, right?" I say, wanting to reassure her.

"Today was just really hard," she whispers. She takes a step back from me. "I'm not hungry, but you can get yourself something for dinner."

"What have you eaten today?" I ask.

"I had lunch," she says as she walks toward her bedroom. "I won't be long. Make yourself at home."

Thinking Danny might get hungry later, I order her a chicken cobb salad and a pizza for myself.

I turn on the TV and switch to a channel that has a baseball game showing. Sitting down on the couch, that gives me a view of the hallway and Danny's room, worry for her fills me.

Something's wrong, and it has nothing to do with work.

Thirty minutes later, when the food is delivered, and there's still no sign of Danny, my worry grows. I force myself not to hover around her and eat some of the pizza.

When an hour has passed, I walk into her room and knock on the bathroom door. "Danny, are you okay?"

She doesn't answer, and it has me pushing the door open. Danny's sitting in the bath, her legs pulled up against her front, while her body shivers as if she's freezing. Crouching next to the tub, I place my hand on her back, and feeling how cold she is, I mutter, "Fuck, Danny!" Getting up, I push my arm under her knees and wrap the other around her back, then I lift her out. I carry her to the bed and set her down, then rush back to the bathroom for a towel.

I've never seen her like this. Can it really be that she's just heartbroken because she's not pregnant?

I dry her body, then wrap the towel around her. Sitting down, I pull her onto my lap and try to rub some warmth into her. "Talk to me."

She shakes her head, letting out a quivering breath.

"Is it because you're not pregnant?" I ask.

Danny nods, and then the tears come again.

"Oh, baby. I didn't know it was so important to you," I murmur, pressing a kiss to her forehead.

I try to comfort her as best I can, and finally, she glances up at me, but then I see a world of pain in her eyes. "I'm sorry I'm such a mess. I'm just struggling to process it."

"That's okay. There's nothing to be sorry for," I reassure her, my voice soft. "Want me to stay the night?"

She nods, then buries her face in the crook of my neck. "God, Ryker," she sobs as if the realization just hit again.

I tighten my arms around her, and hearing her so heartbroken chips away at my own heart.

Fuck, I wish there was a way to make her feel better.

Chapter 12

DANNY

Sitting across from Christopher, I say, "I'm taking tomorrow off."

His eyes snap to mine. "Why?"

I shrug, trying to keep from bursting out in tears as I lie to him. "I need a couple of personal days. The stress is getting to me."

"Do you have anything planned?" he asks.

"I'm going to book into a spa and just relax." I force a smile to my lips. "So, I probably won't answer my phone. Will you be okay handling everything for a day?"

"Of course. You need the rest," Christopher says, a smile curving his lips up.

"Thanks." Getting up, I add, "I owe you."

"You'll have to handle things while I'm on honeymoon, so we're fine."

"A week until the wedding," I murmur. "How do you feel?"

"Impatient as fuck," he chuckles.

We'll all be taking the private jet next Friday evening to San Diego for the wedding. Dash, her mom, and my mom will fly out on Thursday to make sure everything is ready.

"I bet." Giving my brother a smile, I walk out of his office and head back to mine.

It's hard to act as if nothing is wrong. I keep telling myself not to panic… but God… there's a freaking growth in my head.

Cold shivers race over my skin as I walk to my desk. Picking up my bag, I turn to leave when Ryker comes in. His eyebrow raises. "Are you going home?"

"Yeah."

His eyes scan over me. He's been giving me scrutinizing glances since yesterday. It's especially hard lying to him.

"I'm not coming in tomorrow."

He tilts his head at the news. "Why?"

"I'm checking into a spa for the weekend. I just need to unwind."

Relief eases the worry from his face. "That's a good idea. I'm glad you're taking time for yourself."

"So, don't worry if I don't answer my phone," I add.

Ryker closes the distance between us and presses a kiss to my forehead. "I won't. Just let me know the minute you get back. Okay?"

I nod. "Want to come over tonight?"

It will keep me from losing my mind.

"Of course. I just need to stop at my place for a change of clothes."

"Okay. I can grab us dinner on the way home."

"Sounds good," he murmurs, his gaze lovingly sweeping over my face.

Lifting on my toes, I give him a kiss before we walk out of my office. We go our separate ways at the elevators, and instantly the worry streams back.

It's just a biopsy. Nothing huge. They're just going to drill a freaking hole in my head and then rip a piece of the growth off.

Nothing to worry about at all.

―――――――――

Signing myself into the hospital, I hover over the question asking for my next of kin details.

My heart twists painfully as I think of which name to fill in. I don't want my parents to find out something went wrong via a sudden phone call. Christopher just had a lot of his own trauma to deal with.

Pressing the pen to the paper I write, *Tristan Hayes*, thinking he'll be able to handle the shock best out of everyone.

When I'm done with all the paperwork, I'm shown to a private room. VIP status has its perks. At least I don't have to interact with other patients while I wait.

"The biopsy is scheduled for ten am. Make yourself comfortable," the nurse says. I sit down on the bed and stare at the bedside table while she takes all my vitals and wraps hospital bands around my wrist. "There you go. Watch a little TV or take a nap." She gives me an encouraging smile.

"Thank you."

When she leaves, I kick off my shoes and lie back on the bed. I stare up at the ceiling for a couple of minutes.

Maybe I should've told Ryker.

I shun the idea as quickly as it came. I don't want to cause any of my loved ones unnecessary worry.

My phone beeps, and after digging it out of my handbag, I see there's a text from Ryker.

R: Enjoy the spa. Get a lot of rest. Love you.

A sad smile tugs at my lips.

D: I lied. I'm so sorry. I have a growth in my fucking head, and I'm scared to death. God, I wish you were here to hold me and tell me it's going to be okay.

A tear sneaks from my eye as I press delete on what I typed.

D: I will. I love you so much. Thank you for putting up with my mood swings.

I wipe the tear away as Ryker replies.

R: I didn't do much, but I'm here for whatever you need. You don't have to carry everything on your own anymore. I know you're badass, but you can lean on me whenever things become too much.

Another tear spills over my cheek as I soak in his words.

D: I need you. I can't do this on my own.

D: See why I love you so much? There you go sweeping my feet from under me again. Talk to you on Sunday. xox

I turn off my phone and throw it back in my handbag, and then I focus on regaining control over my emotions.

You can do this, Danny.

You just have to.

"Ma'am... ma'am."

A tapping on my arm has me blinking against the bright light above me.

"What's your name?"

"Danny," I grumble.

"Can you remember what day it is?" the voice asks again.

"Uh... Friday?" My sight comes into focus, and I see a nurse next to the bed.

"Can you move your left arm for me?" I do as she asks. "Wiggle your fingers." We go through the same process with my other arm and legs as well.

"How do you feel? Any pain?" she asks.

"Just sleepy," I mumble.

"Okay. Rest a while. Dr. Friedman will be with you shortly."

Minutes later, I feel a hand on my shoulder, and when I open my eyes, Dr. Friedman says, "Hi, Danny. How are you feeling?"

"Okay," I murmur, still a little out of it.

"You're in the recovery room. We'll move you to the ICU soon, where you'll spend the night. It's just for precaution. Okay?"

"Okay." I wet my lips, then ask, "Did you get what you needed?"

Dr. Friedman places his hand on the bed, his eyes locking on mine. A weird sense of dread chases the last of the grogginess away.

"We manage to get a viable sample of the tumor, and I've already sent it to pathology. Everything went well. Get some rest. Okay?"

Slowly, I nod, and soon after the doctor leaves, I drift off to sleep.

––––––––––––––––

I have to wait a couple of days for the results, and with a box of pain meds for the headaches, I'm discharged.

I got a ton of sleep at the hospital, but I'm still exhausted when I get home. I place my overnight bag in my bedroom, then sit down on the edge of the bed.

Somehow… I have to find a way to act as if nothing is wrong. My family and Ryker will pick up on the slightest thing.

I let out a sigh as I slump back on the mattress.

I close my eyes and rest my hands on my stomach, focusing on my breaths.

You don't know if it's bad.

It can be nothing, and with a quick surgery, it can be removed.

It doesn't help you stress about something you have no control over.

Deep breaths.

I keep saying the words until I feel calm, and then I get up to call Ryker.

"Are you home?" he answers after the second ring.

"Yeah, I just got back." Glancing around my place, I ask, "Can I come over?"

"Of course," he murmurs.

"Can you send me the address?" I've only been there once for the home warming three years ago and honestly can't remember how to get there.

"I can always come to pick you up," he offers, which is a huge relief. Dr. Friedman told me not to drive because of the dizzy spells. I'll have to hire a chauffeur this week.

"I'd appreciate that. Should I pack a bag?" I ask, injecting a teasing tone into my voice.

"Definitely. Once I have you here, I'm locking you in my bedroom." His voice drops low, sending a wave of desire through me.

"Mhh… sounds like heaven."

"I'll be right over."

I end the call and empty my bag in the laundry hamper. I pick a couple of suits for the coming week and pack casual clothes and underwear.

RYKER

Walking into Danny's place, I say, "You should have a keycard made for me."

"Yeah? For midnight sexcapades?" she teases.

"Amongst other things," I chuckle. Wrapping my arms around her, I press a kiss to her mouth. "This prince wants quick access, incase his princess is stuck in her tower."

A wide smile stretches over her face. "There you go melting my heart again."

I glance at her luggage, and it has an eyebrow raising. Then I give her a playful look. "Do you plan on staying the week?"

Danny shrugs. "Maybe... maybe not."

I steal another kiss from her before I reach for the luggage. "Let's go."

Once we step into the elevator, I ask, "How do you feel about grilled steaks for dinner?"

"As long as you're the one doing the grilling, I'm all for it."

"Bossy," I grumble.

It looks like the weekend did her a world of good. She's back to her old self again, and it eases the worry that's been gnawing at me the past week.

I drive us to my place, and when I pull up the driveway, Danny frowns. "Did you move?"

"Yeah, last year," I reply.

"How did I not know? Didn't you have a home warming?"

"I'm sure I mentioned it. Christopher and Tristan know," I reply. "And I wasn't in the mood for a party."

Her gaze turns back to the house. "Wow… okay."

When we get out, Danny's eyes roam over the landscaped garden. "Why didn't you mention this place when we were talking about a house in the suburbs?"

"Because I thought you knew."

Danny nods and follows me up the stairs. I unlock the door, and when we step inside, Danny's eyes dart everywhere. "Damn, Ryker," she breathes as she walks toward the living room. "Did Mila and your mom help decorate?"

"No," I chuckle. "Why?"

"Because I expected a man cave... not a home." I watch as she trails her fingers over the back of the leather couch.

I leave the bags and follow after Danny as she explores every room. She stops in the dining room then gasps, "That's gorgeous. Where did you get it?"

"I asked Aria to paint me a piece." Aria's a family friend who's currently studying art.

Danny's eyes widen. "Aria painted that?"

I nod. "She's really talented."

We stare at the artwork. Aria painted two bubbles floating in a sea of color. There's a silhouette of a man in the right bubble and in the left one an outline of a woman.

"It's us," I murmur.

Danny's eyes snap to me. "The silhouettes?"

I nod. "It always felt like you were in a different world. Out of my reach."

Danny glances back at the painting. "I know what you mean."

I take hold of her hand, and linking our fingers, I pull her to the kitchen. "Coffee and tea are in there." I show her where the basics are and then tug her up the stairs to the second floor.

"God, you even had the guest rooms decorated. I'm impressed," she mumbles.

"I get the feeling you totally underestimated me," I mutter.

When we walk into my bedroom, Danny nods. "Yeah… yeah, I did."

Grabbing hold of her, I pick her up and place her on the bed. "Finally," I growl as I crawl over her. "I have you where I've always wanted you."

Danny lets out a chuckle as she lifts her hands to my jaw. "Yeah? In your bed?"

Nodding, I lower my mouth to hers and nip at her lips. I brush my hand over her hair to slip it behind her neck, but then Danny flinches while gasping, "Careful."

I instantly pull away.

She pushes herself up on her elbows. "I… I bumped my head. It's just a little gash. A couple of stitches."

Sitting on the side of the bed, I frown at her. "You got hurt? How? When?" I move forward again. "Let me see."

Danny darts upright and takes hold of my hand to stop me from checking. "It's was a stupid accident. I bumped my head, but I'm okay now." She scoots off the bed and holds her hand out to me. "Let's get those steaks on the grill."

The worry returns full force, and getting up, I take hold of her hand and pull her closer. Staring down at her, I ask, "You're not hiding anything from me, are you?"

She shakes her head, a smile curving her lips. "Of course not."

I lift my other hand to her face and framing her cheek, I lean down and press a tender kiss to her mouth, then I murmur, "You know you can lean on me, right?"

Danny nods, her lips curving more.

"I know you're used to being this badass independent woman, but you have me now.'

She lets go of my hand and wraps her arms around me, resting her cheek against my chest. "I know."

I give her a hug and then pull her out of the room to get started with the food.

Chapter 13

DANNY

My stomach is tight with nerves as I sit in the examination room where I'm waiting for Dr. Friedman.

It's going to be okay.

I haven't had any other dizzy spells, and the medication has helped with the headaches, so I feel optimistic.

Dr. Friedman comes into the room, and he pulls a chair closer, sitting down right in front of me. "Hi, Danny. How are you feeling?"

"Hi," I force a smile to my lips. "Not too bad. No dizzy spells and the pain meds help a lot for the headaches."

"That's good to hear. Let's take out those stitches." He wheels the chair closer, and I sit still while he brushes my hair out of the way and removes the stitches. "There we go. The incision is healing nicely."

He rolls the chair a little back, and when his eyes meet mine, my stomach bottoms out, and my heart instantly beats faster.

"Isn't there a loved one you'd like to have here with you today?" he asks.

I shake my head. "What are the results?"

"Okay... so what you have is called Glioblastoma. It's hard to treat and grows at a rapid pace."

I just stare at him, not sure what it means for me.

"The tumor has tentacles, which are difficult to remove with surgery because it grows into the surrounding brain. We won't know how far it's spread until we go in to look."

"Okay," I murmur, still not sure what it means. "Sorry, but what does all of that mean?"

He clears his throat then says, "Glioblastoma is the most aggressive brain cancer, and even with treatment, the average survival is twelve to eighteen months."

A frown forms on my forehead, the words not sinking in. My voice is tense as I ask, "What are you saying?"

"We can operate, and with radiation and chemotherapy, slow the growth of the tumor, but it will keep coming back. I've taken your case to the board at Cedars-Sinai, and they've given approval for us to go ahead with a vaccine therapy trial if you agree. There are other trials we can look at, but in my opinion, this one has the highest success rate. In some cases, we've been able to prolong life to anything between a year and five years. It's different with each case."

Pins and needles spread over my entire body and my insides begin to tremble as I stare at the doctor.

"I understand you want to know how much time you have left, but these things are never easy to predict. One of the positives is that it won't be a painful death."

Death.

My mind latches onto the word.

"I'm going to die?" My voice is hoarse as my breathing begins to speed up.

"With the treatment, we can give you some extra time," he says, empathy softening his tone.

I shake my head. "But you're telling me I'm going to die. At most, I have five years?" I gasp. "That's what you're saying, right?"

Dr. Friedman nods. "I'm sorry, Danny. No one wants this kind of news. We need to focus on what we can do. I'd like to admit you to Cedars-Sinai today and schedule your surgery for forty-eight hours from now."

"How long will I have if we don't do the surgery?" I ask, my voice toneless.

"Three to six months."

I close my eyes as devastation rips through me. Fisting my hands, I try to slow my breathing. My body jerks as I try to contain the sobs. A deep ache spreads through my soul, and I'm filled with a debilitating sense of loss and fear.

Dr. Friedman places his hand on mine. "Do you have someone who can drive you to Cedars-Sinai?"

I shake my head. "I can't. Not today. My brother's wedding is on Saturday."

"You don't have time to delay the surgery. It's important we get in there as soon as possible," Dr. Friedman says, his voice tensing.

I shake my head again. "I'm going to the wedding. I'll be at Cedars-Sinai on Monday. If I'm going to die, I'm not missing my brother's wedding." My voice grows thick, but I push through, "It will probably be the last time my family and friends will be able to gather together for a happy moment before… I'm gone. I'm not taking that away from them."

Dr. Friedman thinks for a moment, then he nods. "You need to check in on Monday. I'll have them prepare a room for you. We'll perform the procedure first thing Tuesday morning."

"What's the risk?" My voice disappears as heat flushes up my neck and face, and tears blur my vision. I have to clench my jaw to keep the tears back, and it strains my voice as I ask, "Is there a chance I can die during the surgery because then I'd rather take the three to six months?"

How the fuck am I calm enough to ask these questions?

"There's always risk where the brain is involved. I've done many of these surgeries. The possible risks are problems with speech, muscle weakness, vision, and other functions. A blood clot might form, so there's the risk of you suffering a stroke."

God.

Dr. Friedman tightens his grip on my hand as if he's trying to lend me some of his strength. "You're still strong, Danny. Let's fight this and give you more time."

More time.

Time.

God.

Nodding, I clear my throat. "Okay. I'll check into Cedars-Sinai on Monday."

"Great." Our eyes meet, then he says, "I'll do everything I can. We'll go over what the procedure entails then."

My body begins to jerk as sobs rattle up my throat, and it takes everything I have to say, "Thank you."

"Do you have any other questions?"

I shake my head.

"Can I call someone for you?"

I shake my head again.

"Would you like me to prescribe you something for shock?"

"No."

He gives me a comforting smile as he hands me his business card. "It has my personal number on there. Call me if there are any new symptoms like seizures or if the headaches get worse."

"Okay."

"Stay in here as long as you need to. Okay? I don't want you driving in this state."

"I have a chauffeur who can take me home," I murmur.

"That's good."

Dr. Friedman stands up, and it has me rising on trembling legs. He gives my shoulder a squeeze. "I'll see you Monday. Okay?"

I nod. "Okay."

Dr. Friedman's eyes lock on mine. "Enjoy the wedding, Danny." He leaves the room, shutting the door softly behind him.

I stand and stare at the door, unable to move a muscle.

Shit… I'm going to die.

My legs go numb, and I quickly sit down again.

Anger explodes through me – scorching, destructive, and paralyzing.

I'm only thirty-two. Other people get to live well into their eighties. I'm not even halfway through life.

There was still so much I wanted to do.

To love Ryker and be loved by him.

To marry him.

To have his children.

To build a future with him.

I won't be there when my brothers have children of their own.

I gasp as the ache in my soul deepens, and folding my arms around my waist, a devastated wail escapes me. I've never heard a sound like it before. But it's the only way to express how I feel because there are no words.

I'm going to die.

Not in forty years.

I won't be here next Christmas.

God, I might not even make the end of this year.

My body begins to jerk as uncontrollable sobs force their way through me. I cover my face with trembling hands and grief the death sentence that's been handed to me.

The door opens and dropping my hands to my lap, I glance at the nurse as she says, "I'm sorry. I didn't know anyone was in here." She begins to close the door, then pauses. "Are you okay?"

Numbly I shake my head.

"Do you want to be alone?"

My chin begins to quiver as I shake my head again.

She comes inside, and shutting the door, she walks to me. Sitting down next to me, she wraps her arms around me.

Feeling the comfort coming from her, I begin to cry. I lift my arms and cling to her.

"I'm going to die," I whimper, my voice drowning in loss and fear.

"I'm so sorry," she murmurs, her voice warm and compassionate.

"I don't want to die," I sob, my body jerking.

"I know," she whispers.

She pulls back, and when I see her red-rimmed eyes, my chest rattles with dry sobs.

She pulls a tissue from her pocket and wipes the tears from my cheeks as she says, "You still have time. Do everything you've ever wanted to do. Spend time with your loved ones. Live every day to the fullest. Okay?"

I nod.

She tilts her head. "I'll keep you in my prayers."

I nod again.

"Can I call someone for you?"

I shake my head and whisper, "I'm going home now."

"Let me walk you out. Okay?"

I nod again, and when we get up, she wraps her arm around my waist. I pick up my handbag, and somehow my legs manage to move. I keep my head lowered, grateful for the nurse walking with me.

When we reach the exit, I turn to her. "What's your name?"

"Sarah Bailey." Her smile is kind, and her eyes warm.

"Thank you, Sarah."

She gives my arm a squeeze, and as I walk to where the car is parked, I feel her eyes on me.

Chapter 14

DANNY

I didn't go back to the office but instead had the chauffeur drop me off at home. I somehow managed to keep it together long enough to call Christopher. I told him I suddenly came down with the flu and will only be back tomorrow.

Sitting on the couch in the dark while hugging a Kleenex box, I listen to my phone ring for what must be the hundredth time, but I can't bring myself to answer it.

Pulling my laptop closer, I sniffle as I open it and type Glioblastoma in the search space.

I scroll to Wikipedia and begin to read about the tumor. My eyes stop on a specific section, and I keep rereading it.

The typical duration of survival following diagnosis is 12 to 15 months, with fewer than 3 to 7% of people surviving longer than five years. Without treatment, survival is typically three months.

I'm going to die.

I slam the laptop shut and let out a rage-filled scream. My breaths explode over my lips as I get up. I begin to pace the length of my living room and then stop in front of the windows. My eyes dart wildly over all the lights shining from nearby buildings.

This isn't happening.

I slam a fist against the window as a cry rips from me.

This is not happening to me.

I'm only thirty-two.

I finally found the love of my life.

Thinking of Ryker, my lips part on a silent scream as dry sobs begin to shudder through me. I drop to my knees, leaning against the window.

I don't want to die.

My breathing comes out in short, panicked gasps.

What's after life? Heaven? Hell? Nothing?

What happens to me when I die?

The panic and fear flooding me forces me back to my feet.

I've never been a religious person. Religions only span over the last ten thousand years, where the earth is billions of years old, so I could never bring myself to believe in something so short-lived in the grand scheme of things.

Mom once told me my grandmother believed our essence returns to nature. Mom believes it too.

That's not so bad. Right?

I'll become a part of the flowers, the trees, butterflies. I'll still be here in some way.

I latch onto the thought because it's better than nothing. It's better than wondering whether heaven or hell waits on the other side of death.

I'll lose my mind if I have to try and solve the ultimate mystery of life, which I'll soon have to face on my own.

No one will be able to hold my hand once I'm dead. It will just be me, and whatever's on the other side.

Oh God.

I begin to heave and run for the bathroom. My body convulses as I empty my stomach. When there's nothing left to bring up, I slump back against the tub and stare at the wall.

I'm going to die.

At this rate, I'm going to go insane long before I die.

Get up, Danny.

I push to my feet and brush my teeth.

Get your shit together.

The wedding is the day after tomorrow. Just make it through this weekend.

You can lose your mind on Monday.

Lifting my eyes to the mirror, I keep repeating the words until the hopeless loss and fear retreats.

Feeling a little calmer, I walk to the living room. My phone begins to ring again, and glancing at it, I see Ryker's name flashing on the screen.

Needing to hear his voice, I pick up the phone and answer the call.

"Hi," I croak, my voice raw from all the crying.

"Fuck, I was a second away from punching the concierge," he grumbles.

"You're here?" I ask, a numb feeling spreading through my body.

"Yeah. Let me up."

"I don't want to give you the flu."

"Let me up, Daniele," he orders.

"Okay," I whisper, too exhausted to fight.

I slump back on the couch, surrounded by snotty tissues. I pick up the Kleenex box and hug it to my chest as I sniffle.

Hey, at least I have an excuse for why I look like death.

A sob rattles through me, and as I try to swallow it down, a hard lump forms in my throat.

The elevator opens, and when Ryker comes in, I begin to tremble from the effort it takes to not break down again.

He takes one look at me. "God, Danny." Coming over to me, he moves the snotty tissues as if they're nothing and sits down. He wraps an arm around my shoulders and pulls my head to his chest. "Did you get meds?"

I nod as my breath rattles over my lips.

Ryker places his palm on my forehead then says, "You feel warm. Let's get you in comfy clothes and in bed. Have you eaten?"

I shake my head and whisper, "I'm not hungry."

Ryker slips an arm underneath my knees and lifts me to his chest as he gets up. As he carries me to my room, I take a deep breath of him.

God, I'm going to miss how good he smells.

The thought rips through me like a tornado and shuddering, I gasp, unable to stop the tears from falling.

"Oh baby," he murmurs as he sits down on the bed, his arms wrapping tightly around me. "Are you sure it's the flu?"

I nod and struggle to get the words out, "My head..."

"A headache?" he asks before pressing a kiss to my hair.

I have a tumor in my brain, and it's killing me.

Unable to say the words, I can only nod.

Ryker moves me onto the bed. "Where do you keep the meds?"

"Bathroom cabinet," I whisper hoarsely.

RYKER

After I got some painkillers into Danny and helped her change into a pair of sweatpants and a sweater, I press another kiss to her feverish forehead.

"I'll order you chicken soup," I murmur. "Want some tea?"

"Please," she murmurs, her voice sounding as fragile as she looks.

She was fine this morning but looking at her now, it looks the flu is kicking her butt.

Her eyes are swollen, and her face and neck are covered with red blotches, probably from the fever.

I walk to the kitchen and prepare tea for her. Grabbing a bottle of water from the fridge, I carry it back to the room. I set the bottle down on the bedside table and then help Danny sit up so she can have the tea.

I wait for her trembling hands to take hold of the mug, then pull my phone out. I place an order for the soup, then drop the device next to the bottle of water.

Lifting a hand, I bush my palm over the side of her head. "Is there anything else I can get you?"

Danny shakes her head, and when she takes a sip, she sputters and coughs. I quickly grab the tea from her and set it down.

"I hate seeing you like this," I mutter as frustration sweeps through my chest.

Danny lifts her hands to her face, and then a heartbreaking sob bursts from her. Moving closer, I wrap my arms around her and hold her to my chest.

"Oh, baby," I murmur, pressing kisses to her hair. "I'm sorry you're sick." She begins to cry harder, and it rips at my heart. Not knowing what else to do, I just hold her, murmuring, "I love you. I wish I could make you feel better."

She begins to calm down until she just leans against me, soft sobs rippling over her lips, and somehow it guts me even more.

Kicking off my shoes, I pull away from her, just long enough to strip out of my suit. "Move up, babe," I whisper, and when she does, I slip in beside her and then pull her to me. "Try to get some sleep. Okay?"

Danny curls into my side, her whole body shivering. Turning onto my side, I wrap my arms tighter around her, squashing her against my body.

"Will you stay?" she whimpers.

"As long as you need me to."

I hold her until the food is delivered, but I can't get her to eat the soup.

Danny also doesn't fall asleep but instead goes from holding me to crying before calming down again. The night follows the same pattern, and in the early morning hours, I get her to drink some water.

When the sun begins to shine through the windows, I say, "I'll have to head to work soon. Will you be okay, or can I drop you off at your parents' place?"

"I'm just going to try and get some sleep before we leave for San Diego," she answers, her voice raw.

"I'll check in on you during lunch."

Danny nods as she sits up. She lets out an exhausted sigh. "Just take my keycard."

Getting out of bed, I put on my clothes, then go make some coffee for myself and tea for Danny.

We drink it in silence, and when I take the empty mug from her, I say, "I'm going to shoot home so I can shower and get clean clothes and my bag for the weekend. I'll stop at the store for some Gatorade for you. Is there anything else I can get you? Tissues?"

Danny shakes her head.

Leaning over her, I press a kiss to her forehead. "I'll be back soon."

She just stares at the covers, looking like she's been drained of her will to live.

Sitting down again, I place a finger under her chin and nudge her face up. It takes a couple of seconds before her eyes drift to mine.

"I think I should take you to the hospital. You don't look well," I voice my concern.

Her eyes water, and she takes a deep breath. "I just need some sleep."

"Call me the instant you feel worse. Okay?"

When she nods, I lean in and press a kiss to her mouth. I feel her lips tremble, and it makes it hard to pull back.

My gaze locks on hers. "I love you."

Her features tighten, and she closes her eyes as she whispers, "I love you too."

Getting up, I wish I could take the day off, but there's just too much work to do. I grab my phone from next to the bed, and leaning over her, I press another kiss to the top of her head. "I'll be back soon," I say again before I leave so I can go get ready for work.

Chapter 15

DANNY

How do you face death?

How do you live with the fact that your days are numbered – not in years, but in months – days – hours even?

How am I supposed to process any of this?

How am I supposed to just accept that I'm going to die?

I won't get married.

I won't have children of my own.

I won't.

I can't.

I refuse to.

"I refuse to!" The scream echoes through my apartment, the sound sharp and angry.

Getting up from the bed, I run to the living room and grab my laptop. I feel feverish as I open the device and type in, 'Glioblastoma survivors.'

My eyes latch onto the first article.

Ten years.

Oh God, someone has survived ten years!

I find more stories of survival, and with each one I read, it builds my hope back up and forces the fear down.

I spend the entire morning reading survival stories, the treatment they had, what they faced, and how they overcame it.

They have to keep going for checkups every three months, and the risk of the tumor coming back is always there, but they're alive.

One woman even had a baby of her own.

Oh God, there's hope.

If they can survive, then I can fight this as well.

My breathing is fast, and I stop reading, soaking in the hope like the dying person I am.

There's no certainty, but I'll take whatever hope I can get.

Feeling a hell of a lot better, I walk to my room to shower and pack my bag for the weekend.

I'm going to enjoy the wedding with my family and friends. I'm going to have fun and share in Christopher and Dash's happiness.

On Sunday, I'll tell my family, and on Monday, I'll check into Cedars-Sinai. On Tuesday, Dr. Friedman will remove the tumor. I'll do everything he tells me to do.

I'm going to fight this.

I'm going to fight for my happily ever after with Ryker.

I'm going to fight for my unborn children.

I'm going to fight for my life like I've never fought before.

I'm not giving up.

Not this Hayes. Not today. Not tomorrow. Not ever.

I will fight until my last breath.

I step into the shower and go through my routine. I wash my hair, taking care with the healing incision. When I'm done drying off my body, I lather myself in lotion.

For the first time in my life, I'm mindful of every single thing I do. I enjoy every second.

I'm going to live my life to the fullest.

I pick a cute top that hangs off my shoulders and pair it with black jeans. I slip on my favorite heels and then take my time putting on my make-up.

I'm spraying on some perfume when I hear the elevator open.

Picking up my diamond-studded earrings, I'm busy putting them on when Ryker walks into the bedroom. He comes to a sudden stop, and then his lips part.

"Damn, you look fucking hot."

"Thank you," I grin at him.

"What happened? You looked like you were dying this morning, and now you're ready to kick ass."

His words stab at my still-fragile heart, but I shove the feeling aside. "All the love and tender care you gave me did the trick," I say. I place my hand on his arm as he leans in for a kiss.

"God, you smell good," he murmurs before deepening the kiss.

I wrap my arms around his neck, taking in the feel of his strong arm around me. When his fingers brush over my neck and shoulder, my skin sizzles to life under his touch. Feeling his tongue stroke against mine. His lips kneading mine. I take it all in, and I bask in every second.

When Ryker pulls back, I smile wide at him. "I love you, Ryker West. So much."

His lips curve up, and his eyes fill with emotion. "Same, babe. Same." He steps back, his eyes roaming over me again. "Damn, I have one hell of a sexy girlfriend. How fucking lucky am I?"

I let out a chuckle as I take hold of his hand and ask, "Have you eaten?"

"No, I rushed over to check on you. Work is a little crazy."

"Let's grab something to go and get back to the office."

"You sure?" He asks, his gaze scrutinizing me.

"The sooner we get everything done, the sooner this weekend can start." Placing my free hand on his solid chest, I ask, "Did you change our reservations from two rooms to one?"

He nods. "Of course."

"Good," I murmur before I wrap my arm around his neck and pull him down for another kiss.

RYKER

Sitting on the plane, surrounded by some of our friends and family, it's hard to not take hold of Danny's hand.

Leaning over, I whisper, "Until when are we keeping our relationship a secret?"

She gives me a playful smile, then leans in until her breath fans over my ear. Her teeth tug at my earlobe, almost making me groan. "You can tell everyone whenever you want to."

Pulling back, our eyes lock. When I see she's serious, I take hold of Danny's hand, and linking our fingers, I mutter, "Thank fuck, it's really hard not touching you." Leaning in again, I press a kiss to her mouth, and I'm rewarded with a beautiful smile from her.

"I can't believe what I'm seeing. Are you dating?" Noah, my cousin, suddenly asks.

I nod, a grin spreading over my face. "She finally gave in to my charms."

Danny lets out a burst of laughter. "He's lying. I had to get him drunk, and then I took advantage of him."

Everyone begins to laugh.

"Congrats, guys," Carla, Noah's wife, says.

There's a chorus of congratulations from everyone on board.

When we touch down in San Diego, I keep hold of Danny's hand as we leave the plane. I lead her to the nearest van. The hotel sent over a couple to collect us from the airport.

Once we're seated, I place my arm around her shoulders, and when she leans her head against me, I press a kiss to her hair.

This will be the first time we're at a function together as a couple, and it fills my chest with pride.

Yeah, I'm the man who got Daniele Hayes.

I tighten my hold on her, and ducking my head, I whisper, "You do know I'm never letting you go?"

Danny tilts her head back, a happy smile on her face. "Yeah?"

"Yeah." Lifting my other hand to her jaw, I keep her face in place as I claim her mouth. I have to remind myself we're not alone and break the kiss way before I've had my fill.

When we arrive at the hotel, I get the keycard for our room, and the second I shut the door behind us, I grab hold of Danny and yank her to me.

My mouth finds hers, and the kiss quickly turns desperate. Our breaths fill the air, and once again, the kiss feels different, just like the one in Danny's bedroom. It's as if she's pouring everything into the kiss. She's not thinking of anything but me, and it only makes me focus more on her.

When we finally pull apart, Danny's eyes are shining like sapphires.

I shake my head slowly, "Something's different."

Her lips curve up. "I'm just not taking you for granted."

"You never did."

Danny lifts her hands to my jaw, her eyes filling with love. "You're a dream come true, Ryker. I want you to know that every second we're together."

I press another quick kiss to her mouth. "You're my dream come true, as well."

We stand, holding each other.

"I'm going to marry you one day." The words slip out before I even had time to process them.

Her smile widens. "Yeah?"

I nod, sure of the fact. "Yeah."

"Danny West," she whispers, and hearing the words makes my heart expand impossibly with love for her.

"You're the only woman I'll ever love," I admit. "It's always been you, and nothing will change that."

Emotion washes over her face, and her eyes begin to tear up. I figure it's because of what I said, and don't read too much into it.

"You're the only man I'll love." Her chin quivers, and then she whispers, "Until the day I die."

Wrapping her against my chest, I say, "Luckily, that's still forty to fifty years away."

Danny lets out a soft sob, and when I try to pull back, she tightens her hold around my neck. "I'm just emotional. Just hold me."

I tighten my arms around her again, and lifting her against my body, I walk deeper into the room until I get to the couch. Sitting down, I pull her onto my lap.

My phone vibrates, and pulling it out of my pocket, I see there's a text from Tristan.

T: Room number. Now.

"Tristan found out we're dating," I say as I reply to the text.

Danny shoots up off my lap. "Let me talk to him."

Rising to my feet, I shake my head. "Don't worry about it."

There's a hard knock at the door, and when panic flashes over Danny's face, I say, "I've got this. Don't worry."

I open the door and stand to the side so Tristan can come in. He settles a dark frown on me, then growls, "My fucking sister?"

"Tristan –," Danny begins to say.

Tristan's eyes slant to her as he snaps, "You keep quiet. This is between Ryker and me."

I shake my head. "Don't talk to her like that." It draws his attention back to me. We stare at each other for a moment, and I see the anger brewing in his eyes. "I love, Danny."

His features tighten as he begins to slowly shake his head.

"Tristan," I mutter. "We fucking love each other. You know what it's like. Could you have stayed away from Hana?"

He takes a deep breath, his gaze snapping from me to Danny, then back to me. "How long has this been going on?"

"This?" I narrow my eyes on him. "We're in a relationship. Nothing you do or say is going to change that."

"Is that right?" he asks, fisting his hands at his sides.

I know my friend. He has a volatile nature, and the last thing I want now is to get into a fight with him.

Locking eyes with him, I say, "What's your problem? I love Danny. You know I'll be good to her. Why is this an issue?"

My words get through to him, and he takes a step back, sucking in a deep breath. "Why didn't you tell me? Either of you?"

"We were going to tell you this weekend," Danny murmurs.

Tristan's eyes lock on mine, and it has me saying, "Because I never thought anything would come of it. We've only been together five weeks."

He stares at me for a solid minute, then says, "You better not break her heart."

"I don't have a death wish," I mutter.

My comment draws a chuckle from Tristan. "Nah, I'd just break your legs."

Shaking my head, I smile at him. "So, we're good?"

"Yeah, we're good." He lets out a sigh. "At least I know I can trust you with Danny." He pulls a disgruntled face. "And you're better than all the other dickheads she tried to date."

"Thank God," Danny mumbles as she sits down. "All this testosterone is giving me a headache."

Chapter 16

DANNY

Standing to the side, dressed in a one-shoulder, baby blue tulle gown, my eyes go to where Ryker is sitting next to his mom while Christopher and Dash are saying their vows.

As if Ryker can feel my eyes on him, his gaze flicks to mine, and then the corner of his mouth curves up.

There's a sudden sharp pain in my head, and I quickly glance down at the flowers in my hands. Closing my eyes. I breathe through the ache until it becomes a dull throbbing.

Just two more days, Danny.

Just two days.

Miss Sebastian, who's Dash's godmother, pronounces them husband and wife, and cheers break out.

I force a smile to my lips and lifting my head, I watch as Christopher tilts Dash in his arms, kissing the hell out of her.

My smile quickly turns real, and laughter bubbles from me.

The guests move to the reception hall, while the wedding party stays behind to take a couple of photos.

Christopher, Tristan, and I pose for a photo, and just as the camera flashes, my vision blurs. My legs go numb, and I grab hold of Tristan's arm. He instantly places an arm around my waist.

"You okay?"

I nod as I blink and slur, "Just a... little dizzy... from being... in the sun."

He rubs a hand over my back, then says, "Danny's taking a break." Tristan helps me over to a chair, and every step shudders through my body as if I can't estimate where the ground is, and my steps are too hard.

"What's wrong?" Mom calls out.

"She's just a little dizzy. Go on with the photoshoot," Tristan answers, and then he crouches in front of me. His eyes sharpen on my face. "You're pale. Do you want something to drink?"

I shake my head, not sure I'll be able to keep it in. "I just... need to sit... for a moment. I'll be fine."

Tristan moves to the chair next to me, and then he begins to draw patterns on my back. He always did it when we were kids, and I'd have to guess what he's writing.

I focus on his finger, and then my lips curve up. "I love you too."

"Haven't lost the touch," he chuckles.

Dad walks over to us and sits down on my other side. "You okay, princess?"

"Yeah," I murmur.

"I saw you and Ryker holding hands," Dad says.

"Yeah... we're dating. I love... him."

I begin to worry that Dad will pick up on how stilted my speech is.

"Love?" Dad asks. "When did this happen?"

I sit forward, resting my chin on my palm. "It's been... coming since he started... at Indie Ink."

"You really love him?" Tristan asks.

"I do. With all.... my heart."

Dad leans forward, so I have to look at him. "How does he feel about you?"

"He loves me, Daddy. We're happy... together."

Only then does Dad relax a little. "That's all that matters, I suppose."

If I didn't have to worry about dying, I would've been a nervous wreck telling my family I'm dating Ryker.

I couldn't care less now.

I take a deep breath and get up, testing my legs. When they hold, I say, "Come on. Let's get the photos... over with so we can go party."

It takes another thirty minutes before we're making our way to the reception hall. I head straight for the main table and sit down with a sigh.

Reaching for a glass, I pour myself some water and down it in one go.

"You okay?" Ryker asks as he crouches next to my chair.

My lips curve up, and leaning over, I press a kiss to his mouth. "Yeah. Just tired. As soon as they're done... with the speeches, I'll come to sit by you."

"Okay." He reaches up and tucks some of my hair behind my ear.

Mom and Dad head our way, and Dad stops to talk to Ryker while Mom plops down next to me. "So, you and Ryker?"

My eyes lock on Mom's, and smiling, I say, "Yeah, he's... the one."

Mom tilts her head. "Are you okay, sweetheart?"

No, Momma. Far from.

I nod. "Just tired."

She places her hand on mine and gives it a squeeze. "At least we can sit for a while now."

With Mom holding my hand, my eyes go back to Ryker.

I have to tell him tonight.

I hear Ryker say, "Yes, Uncle Carter. Of course."

"Stop grilling him," I chuckle.

Dad shoots me a playful glare. "Just because he's my best friend's son doesn't mean I'm going to take it easy on him."

I begin to laugh, and then Christopher and Dash come into the hall. Everyone begins to cheer, and for the next hour, I get to relax as we listen to one speech after the other.

After Christopher and Dash open the dance floor, I watch as they walk to the stage. He taps on the microphone then says, "We have one last announcement to make, and then you can all enjoy the night." Christopher waits until he has everyone's attention, then he looks at Dash. "Ready?"

She nods, and then they both say, "We're having a baby!"

My lips instantly curve into a happy smile, and I clap my hands along with everyone else.

Then reality hits.

Getting up, I quickly walk to where the restrooms are, and once I'm in a stall, my breaths begin to rush over my lips.

God, what if I don't make it? What if I'm gone by the time their baby is born?

The thought sends a devastating ache through me, and I gasp as I fight to keep the tears back.

Calm down, Danny. You're going to fight. You'll still be here when their baby is born.

"Shh…" I grind my teeth as I fight for control over my rampant emotions. "Shh…"

It takes a couple of minutes for me to calm down, and then I suck in a deep breath, lifting my chin.

You're going to congratulate them. You're going to smile.

You can do this.

―――――――――

RYKER

My eyes are glued to Danny, where she laughs at something Dash just said.

179

Mom pats my leg, then says, "Go ask her to dance."

I turn my head to Mom. "I'll ask her in a minute. First, I want to dance with you."

A smile spreads over Mom's face as she gets up from the chair.

"Where are you going?" Dad asks her.

"To dance with our son, seeing as your butt is glued to the chair," Mom sasses Dad.

Dad gets up and grabs hold of Mom's hand. I let out a burst of laughter as he drags her to the dance floor. Turning my gaze back to Danny, I watch as Uncle Rhett pulls her close for a dance.

There's a happy smile on Danny's face, and I know it's because of her godfather. He spins her suddenly, and she lets out a burst of laughter. "Uncle Ledge!"

A smile curves my lips. She's always called him that, and I still don't know why.

Uncle Rhett steers her in my direction, and I get up when they reach the table. Then his eyes lock with mine, and I know I'm in for another grilling session.

"So... Carter tells me you're dating my princess?" he asks as he sits down. I wait for Danny to take a seat before I lower myself back to my chair.

Before I can answer, Danny says, "Don't you start as well, Uncle Ledge."

"Start what?" he asks her, a way too innocent expression on his face.

His eyes lock on me again, and it has me saying, "Yes, we're dating. I'm serious about Danny. I love her. I'll take good care of her," I get through everything in one go.

Uncle Rhett begins to laugh. "I actually wanted to say congrats, but okay."

I let out a burst of laughter. "Sure."

Mom comes back to the table and sits down next to her brother. "Are you giving my son a hard time?"

"I wouldn't dare," Uncle Rhett grumbles.

Mom leans forward, looking at Danny. "You look beautiful, Danny."

"Thanks, Aunt Mia."

Danny looks a little nervous, and it has me reaching for her hand. I link my fingers with hers, and it earns me a smile.

Mom's eyes narrow on Danny, and her smile begins to fade. It kicks my heartbeat up, but then Mom asks, "Is everything okay, Danny?"

My gaze instantly snaps to Danny's face.

She just laughs the concern away. "Still recovering from the flu."

I let out a breath and relax again.

When I Look At You by Miley Cyrus begins to play, and I get up. "Dance with me?" I ask Danny.

Her smile brightens as she gets up and follows me to the dance floor. I pull her against my chest and wrap my arms around her. Our eyes meet as the lyrics fill the air.

"You look breathtakingly beautiful," I murmur. The blue of the dress makes her eyes pop even more.

"You look handsome yourself, Mr. West." Danny wraps her arms around my neck, and slowly we sway to the music.

"Are you enjoying the wedding?" I ask.

She nods. "I'm glad everything turned out perfect for them."

We spend another two hours with our family and friends before we call it a night.

After saying goodnight, Danny and I head up to our room. Once we've showered and changed into comfortable clothes, Danny walks out on the balcony and stares at the dark ocean. I wrap my arms around her, and she leans back against my chest.

"Today was a good day," she murmurs.

"Yeah," I agree.

Danny takes a deep breath and then pulls away. She tugs me back inside toward the living room. "There's something I have to tell you."

"Okay."

I sit down next to her and turn my body toward hers.

Danny takes hold of my hand, and a smile wavers around her lips as she presses a kiss to my lips. Her eyes meet mine, and she just stares at me.

"What do you want to talk about?" I ask, linking our fingers.

She glances down, and I watch as she swallows. When her eyes meet mine again, and I see the tears in hers, a frown begins to form on my forehead.

"Hey," I murmur.

"This is really hard," she says, and then a tear falls. She swipes it away, taking a deep breath.

Worry bleeds through me, and before I can ask anything, Danny closes her eyes, and her voice sounds strained as she says, "I have a tumor in my head."

My heart tightens into a fist.

"It's... it's..." She sucks in a quivering breath. "Glioblastoma," she squeezes the word out.

My lips part, and I suck in a breath as the word rips a gaping hole through my life. I know what it is. I know what it means. Mom works in a hospice.

I suck in another breath, and then I begin to shake my head. "No."

Danny doesn't open her eyes as more tears begin to fall.

And then everything starts to fall into place.

The headaches.

The dizzy spells.

The weekend at the spa.

Her being emotional.

Her bumping her head.

The flu.

The realization shudders through me like a devastating earthquake.

Christ. No.

I pull my hand away from hers as I begin to shake uncontrollably.

I lift my hands and frame Danny's face. She opens her eyes, and then I see it. The fear.

My body moves forward, and I grab her to me as I begin to shake my head.

Her body trembles as she says, "There are treatments. I'm having surgery on Tuesday. I've looked into it, and there are survivors. I'm going to fight."

I begin to nod, grasping onto the fragile hope while my heart shatters into a million pieces.

I'd like to think I'm strong enough to handle anything life throws my way.

But not this.

I can't watch the woman I love die.

I can't.

The shaking in my body grows, and I hold Danny tighter to me.

"I'm going to fight," she whispers.

I nod again, unable to say anything.

Then it really starts to sink in, like a dead weight pulling me under a wave of grief.

My body jerks as the first tear falls. I clench my jaw and try to swallow the devastation down.

I can't lose Danny.

God, I just got her.

My body jerks again, and it has Danny tightening her arms around me. Then she whispers, "I'm so sorry. If I had known, I never would've started a relationship with you."

Her words have me pulling back. When our eyes meet and she sees my tears, Danny gasps for air as she begins to cry.

Another tear rolls down my cheek as I say, "This doesn't change how I feel about you. I'm just struggling to process it."

Using my thumbs, I brush her tears away while my own fall. Her eyes meet mine again, and then she shakes her head. "I'm scared…" Her body begins to jerk as sobs rip through her. "I'm so scared, Ryker."

I pull her back to my chest and engulf her with my body.

I'm scared too.

Clearing my throat, my voice is hoarse as I say, "I'm here. I've got you."

Danny shakes her head and lifting her face, I hate seeing the naked fear etched into her beautiful features. "The odds aren't good. If I die…" She presses a hand to her chest. "If I die… what happens then? What happens to me? Where do I go? You won't be there."

My tears fall faster as the ground opens beneath me, and I sink to the lowest bowels of hell.

I have to take a breath, and my voice is strained as I say, "You won't go anywhere. If the worst happens, you'll stay right here with me." I take another breath and let it out slowly, trying to keep my shit together for her. "You'll always be a part of me, Danny. You'll live in my heart. I'll fucking rip half my soul out to make space for yours."

Every muscle in my face hurts from fighting to not give in to the grief, the gut-wrenching destruction, the devastating despair.

Danny regains control over her emotions while mine spirals into a chaotic mess.

"I'm going to fight," she says. "There are survivors who have lived with it for ten years. I can do that as well."

I begin to nod, hope warring against the cold hard truth.

Danny lifts her hand to my jaw, and her face begins to crumble, but again she reins it in. "I'm so sorry."

I shake my head as everything suddenly stills inside me.

This isn't about me.

This is about Danny.

"There's nothing to be sorry for," I manage to murmur. My mind begins to race. "I'll talk to Aunt Leigh. She might know of a specialist."

Danny shakes her head. "I've looked into Dr. Friedman and Cedars-Sinai. They've made a lot of progress with vaccine therapy. Most of the survivors that have lived past the ten-year mark… it was because of the vaccine trial. I'm going to stay with Dr. Friedman."

God.

I tilt my head, a frown deepening on my forehead. "When did you find out?"

"Thursday."

I clench my jaw when I remember the state she was in.

I should've listened to my gut.

I close my eyes at the stab of disappointment in myself.

"Ryker," Danny whispers.

Opening my eyes, I focus on her face.

She glances down and takes a deep breath before she looks up again. "You're twenty-five. I don't want this to be your future."

I instantly begin to shake my head. "Don't even go there. There's no way I'm letting you go. We're in this together, no matter the outcome."

A sob flutters over her lips as she looks down again. "I want you to be happy." Her voice disappears, and she swallows hard before she continues, "You deserve to be with a woman who can give you a future."

God, my brave love.

Lifting my hands to the sides of her neck, I lean forward and force her to look at me. "And you're that woman. I love you. There will never be anyone else. Never. You, Daniele Hayes, are the only woman I'll ever love. No matter what you say, no matter how hard you try to push me away, I won't leave you. Get that?"

Her face crumbles as she moves forward, burrowing against my chest. I hold her as tight as I can.

Then she whispers, "I'm going to fight for us."

I begin to nod. "Do that, babe. Give it your all. If anyone can beat this, it's you."

We hold onto each other for a couple of minutes, then Danny asks, "How am I going to tell my parents, my family?"

"If you can't, then I will."

She shakes her head. "I have to."

"Then I'll be there right next to you."

"Ryker," she whimpers, and the fear is now so clear in her voice, I'm fucking angry at myself for not hearing it before.

"I've got you." I press a kiss to her hair. "I wish I could trade places with you."

My words make Danny pull away, and then she begins to shake her head as some kind of realization washes over her face. Her voice is drenched in heartache as she says, "That is the only thing worse than me dying. Don't ever say that again." We stare at each other, and then she sobs, "I'm so sorry for doing this to you. God, I'm so sorry, Ryker."

I frame her face again and lean in close to her. I press my mouth to her quivering lips then murmur, "You're going to beat this, Danny. For us."

She begins to nod again. "I'm going to fight with everything I have."

Somehow I manage to form a smile around my lips. "I'll be there every step of the way. Take whatever strength you need from me. Strip me fucking bare, just don't give up."

Chapter 17

DANNY

Ryker and I stay up all night, and there's nothing left of my heart from seeing how hard the news has hit him.

He just sits and stares at me, and the next moment he'll yank me to his chest while his body shakes.

Seeing his tears… that's the killer.

I've never seen Ryker cry before.

His jaw clenches again, and he shakes his head. His eyes lift to mine, and they're dark with grief.

It makes a new fear bleed through me. My loved ones are only going to see death when they look at me.

I begin to shake my head as a lump pushes up my throat. "Don't look at me like that." A sob escapes me. "I'm not dead yet."

"Fuck, Danny," he growls as he pulls me against his chest. "I'm sorry. I'm just trying to make sense of it all."

"I know," I sniffle. "I just can't stand seeing you grieve for me while I'm still here."

He presses kisses to the side of my head. "I'm sorry."

I can hear the sorrow in his voice. I feel it in his body.

Pulling free, I get up as my breaths keep coming faster. I place a hand on my chest as desolation soaks into my bones.

I walk out onto the balcony, then back into the living room. It feels as if I'm being hunted, death nipping at my heels.

"Danny," Ryker says as he rises to his feet.

I shake my head as I begin to gasp for air, and then a wail rips out of me as I sink down to the floor. I cover my face as gasps burst from me, paralyzing fear and sorrow swallowing me whole.

I feel Ryker's arms slip under me. He lifts me to his chest and then sits down with me on his lap.

His body becomes a solid wall. The shaking fades, and then I feel his strength as he says, "I've got you, Daniele. I've got you. You can break, and I'll pick up all the pieces. Just don't give up. Okay?"

I nod as I empty myself, every tear filled with the frightening fact that no matter how hard I fight, I might not be able to beat this thing.

Finally, I manage to regain control over my emotions, and a numbness sinks into my heart and soul.

With my head resting against Ryker's chest, my body shudders every couple of minutes as lost sobs drift over my lips.

Ryker takes hold of my jaw and nudges my face up so I'll look at him. His eyes are filled with love, and then his lips curve up. "Fuck, you're beautiful. I love you so much."

My eyes lock with his, and not finding the despair in them makes me feel better.

"My badass Danny," he murmurs before pressing a tender kiss to my mouth.

I've managed to get my shit together… again.

Waiting for my family to meet me in our room, my leg keeps jumping. I stand up and walk out onto the balcony, my body tense.

How am I going to tell them?

It was so hard breaking the grim news to Ryker. But Dad… Mom… my brothers… Aunt Jamie… Uncle Rhett? How?

Ryker's arms slip around me, and his chest presses against my back. Solid. Filled with strength. Right now, he's the only thing keeping me standing.

"If you can't tell them, just give me the sign, and I'll take over," he murmurs.

I nod and whisper, "Thank you."

His arms tighten around me, and he presses a kiss to the side of my neck. "Just take hold of my hand, or slap me, anything. Okay?"

I nod, and then a knock at the door has my body freezing. I can't make myself move as Ryker goes to open the door.

"Hey, I got a text from Danny?" Christopher asks.

I close my eyes, hating that I couldn't give him more time to at least enjoy his honeymoon.

"Yeah, come in," Ryker says.

"Did something happen?" Christopher asks, but before he can answer, I hear my parents' laughter.

I try to memorize the sound.

Taking a deep breath, I turn around and see that Uncle Rhett and Aunt Jamie are with them. Tristan comes in behind them, and then Ryker shuts the door. Aunt Jamie is Mom's younger sister. She filled the role of my parent before Dad found us. That's a whole different story, though.

"Is this where the two of you tell us you're engaged?" Dad asks as he sits down.

Mom grins at me, and then her smile begins to fade.

Tristan doesn't even sit down, his eyes narrowing on me. "What's going on, Danny?"

I take a deep breath and shake my head.

God. Give me strength.

Ryker comes toward me, and wrapping his arm around my waist, he presses a kiss to my temple, then whispers, "I'm here."

I nod and swallow hard. Lifting my eyes to Christopher's, I say, "I'm sorry. I tried to give you as much time as I could."

He shakes his head as he rises to his feet. "What are you talking about?"

Mom begins to shake her head. "No." She gets up as her breathing speeds up. "No."

Aunt Jamie's face pales as she glances between Mom and me. "What, Della?"

Mom barely gets the word out. "Mom." Referring to my grandmother, who passed away from cancer. Aunt Jamie was still young back then, so I don't know if she remembers much.

"What's going on?" Dad asks, darting up.

Mom begins to cry, her face distorting. "Tell me it's not what I think it is," she begs.

I try to take a deep breath, my eyes locked on Mom. "I'm so sorry."

"What?" Dad shouts.

"I have Glioblastoma," I force the words through gritted teeth.

Dad shakes his head. "What's that?"

I grab hold of Ryker's hand, unable to say the words.

Ryker clears his throat, then says, "Danny has a tumor in her brain. It's the most aggressive brain cancer. She's scheduled for surgery on Tuesday morning."

Mom lets out a cry, and then she rushes to me while Aunt Jamie covers her mouth with her hands.

When Mom grabs hold of me, I close my eyes and fight to keep it together. Her fingers grip hold of my sweater as she begins to gasp for air, and all I can do is stand frozen.

"What?" Dad gasps. "What are you saying?"

"There is a treatment plan in place. It's had positive results," Ryker continues.

"Ryker!" Uncle Rhett shouts. "What the fuck does it mean for Danny?"

"There's only a five percent survival rate after five years."

"Christ," Tristan hisses. "Fucking fuck." Then he snaps, "No, there has to be something we can do."

196

"I'm so sorry," I whisper.

Dad makes a painfilled sound, something between a growl and a sob. "Are you saying Danny's dying?"

"No," Ryker bites out. "She's just sick. With treatment, she can fight this. She's not dying."

"Can't Leigh help?" Uncle Rhett asks.

"Her field is cardiothoracic. Not brain cancer," Ryker answers.

Mom begins to calm down, and as she pulls away, she stammers, "I... I... Not my baby."

I can't bring myself to look at my family. Sorrow drowns out all the light. Fear is palpable in the air.

I tighten my hold on Ryker's hand as tight as I can, and it has him stepping in behind me. I feel his chest rise and fall against my back and try to match my quivering breaths to his.

"What's most important is that Danny's still here," Ryker says, his voice firm and filled with the strength I need to just cope. "There's hope. She's going to fight this, and she needs every bit of support and strength we can give her."

"But..." Christopher groans. "But..."

I raise my eyes, and then I'm hit with a wave of raw heartache, unlike anything I've ever experienced. Dad looks like he's stuck in a daze. Uncle Rhett keeps shaking his head. Mom's… just broken. Aunt Jamie has tears running down her pale face.

I glance at Christopher, who looks at me like I'm a ghost. I try to take a step back, but Ryker's body stops me.

Then I look at Tristan, and I gasp when I see the pain etched into his features, a tear spiraling down his cheek.

"I'm so sorry," I whimper.

Tristan moves forward, and then he grabs hold of me, yanking me away from Ryker. His arms lock around me, his grip bordering on painful. Then my brother says, "Shh… we'll find a way to get through this."

I nod against his chest. "I'm going to fight."

I feel Tristan press a kiss to my head. "And I'll be right there fighting with you. Okay? If you need anything, you tell me."

I nod again.

Tristan pulls back only for Christopher to take hold of me. I feel his body shake, and bringing a hand to his back, I try to comfort him. "It's going to be okay," I whisper. "I want you to go on your honeymoon."

Christopher shakes his head. "Not a chance of that happening. I'm not leaving you when you need me most. The honeymoon can wait until after you're better."

I pull back while nodding. "Thanks, Christopher."

Knowing I have to, I walk to where Dad's still standing in a trance. I try to force a smile to my lips. "Daddy."

His eyes lower to mine, and it's the first time in my life where all I see is fear. His movements are stilted as he lifts a hand to my shoulder, and then he whispers, "Princess."

"I'm so sorry, Daddy. I wish... I wish..." My breaths speed up, and I begin to shiver from how much it hurts.

Dad takes a deep breath, and then his features harden. I watch as he reins in his pain, and then he asks, "Who's the doctor?"

"Dr. Friedman. I have to check in tomorrow morning at Cedars-Sinai."

"Do you have his contact number?" Dad asks.

I nod and walking to my handbag, I take the business card from it and then hand it to Dad.

I watch as Dad takes his phone out and dials Dr. Friedman's number.

Chapter 18

RYKER

Uncle Carter must have the phone on speakerphone because the next minute, we all hear, "Dr. Friedman speaking."

"Doctor, It's Carter Hayes, Danny Hayes' father," Uncle Carter says, his eyes not leaving Danny. "She just told us the news. Explain everything to me."

"Mr. Hayes, I'm glad to hear Danny told you. I was worried about her doing this on her own." Dr. Friedman clears his throat, then he continues, "With the last MRI, the growth was roughly the size of half a fist. Glioblastoma is a tricky thing, though. It has tentacles that grow into the surrounding brain, and it's hard to get it all out. That means it keeps coming back."

"What treatment options are we looking at?" Uncle Carter asks.

No one makes a sound as Dr. Friedman explains, "First we'll remove as much as we can of the tumor. During the surgery, I'll inject twenty injections of what we like to refer to as Trojan horse therapy. We take the common cold virus… adenovirus, which is highly infectious, and strip it apart, so it doesn't spread like wildfire. We've added a herpes virus DNA into it, so when we administer the injections, the virus infects the remaining tumor. Twenty-four hours later, we'll give Danny a Valtrex treatment, which will kill the herpes, and along with it, the tumor."

"So, you can kill it all?" Uncle Carter asks, hope making his voice hoarse.

"We're going to try. Danny will also have to receive daily radiation treatments for six weeks, and after that chemotherapy for six months."

"Fuck," I mutter, hearing what she'll have to endure.

"But like I said, in most cases, the tumor returns," Dr. Friedman ends his explanation.

"Are there cases where it doesn't return?" Uncle Carter asks.

"I have one patient who just made the eleven-year mark," Dr. Friedman answers.

"So, there's a chance this could work?" Aunt Della asks. "Sorry, I'm Della, Danny's mom. My mother passed away because of Glioblastoma."

"There is always a chance. We keep looking for new ways. Glioblastoma is not a curable disease, though. We can only try to manage it." Dr. Friedman pauses, then he asks, "Is Danny with you?"

Danny clears her throat. "I'm here."

"You're checking in tomorrow morning, right?" Dr. Friedman asks.

"Yes."

"Try to be here at seven am. There's a lot we need to do before surgery."

"I'll be there," Danny says.

"Is there anything else I can help with?" Dr. Friedman asks.

"Do you know who I am, doctor?" Uncle Carter asks.

"Yes, Sir. I do."

"I'll pay anything. I'll start whatever foundation you want me to. Make Danny your priority. Please," Uncle Carter says, his voice hoarse.

"I'll do everything in my power to help her," Dr. Friedman replies.

When the call ends, it all still feels hopeless.

I can see on everyone's faces they feel the same.

I walk to Danny and wrap my arm around her waist. "I think we should get back to LA as soon as possible."

Danny nods. "Yeah, I have things to get in order before the surgery."

Uncle Carter makes another call so they can get the private jet fueled and ready.

Danny presses to my side as she says, "I can't tell the rest of the family and our friends. This was hard enough. Could you all just spread the word?"

No one replies as they just stare at Danny with grief-stricken expressions.

"Please." Danny's voice is tight.

"I'll tell everyone," I say when it's clear her family's too in shock to think straight.

Taking my phone out, I begin to create a group chat, and it takes a couple of minutes to add everyone who needs to be told. Not wanting to send a text, I decide on a voice clip.

I walk to the bedroom, and shutting the door behind me, I press record. "Hey, everyone. I'm sorry for telling you this way, but to call everyone is not an option. Danny's sick. She has Glioblastoma. It's… it's brain cancer. The worst kind. There are treatment plans in place. I'll keep you up to date via this chat with any progress she makes." I send the message needing a moment to just breathe, and then I start the next voice clip. "Danny's strong. She's going to fight this. There is hope. She's obviously not taking it well, none of us are. If you reach out to her, don't treat her like she's dying." My voice breaks, and after clearing my throat, I say, "She's checking in to Cedars-Sinai tomorrow. The surgery is Tuesday. Like I said, I'll send regular updates via this chat."

I watch as our family and friends mark it as read, and then the bubbles begin to jump like crazy.

I exit the app, and before I can turn off my phone, it begins to ring. Seeing it's Mom, I answer, "Hey, Mom."

I hear Mom take a deep breath, and then her calm voice comes over the line. "Hey, how are you holding up?"

"I'm not," I admit. "Not at all."

"You need to be strong for Danny, and I'll be strong for you," Mom says.

Closing my eyes, I'm overwhelmed with the urge to break down.

"Deep breaths, Ryker. Take deep breaths. There's a long road ahead of you. Don't look at it as a death sentence for Danny. Make every day special and comfortable for her."

"Okay," I murmur.

"She's still here. That's what matters. Danny's still here," Mom says, her voice soft and filled with empathy.

"I know."

"I'll meet you at the hospital tomorrow. Okay?"

I begin to nod. "Thanks, Mom."

"You can do this," Mom encourages me.

To think my mother deals with this on a daily basis. God.

The thought gives me a burst of strength. If Mom can do it, so can I.

"I love you, Ryker. I'm here."

"Love you," I whisper.

After the call, I don't answer the texts but close my eyes and take deep breaths.

You can do this.

Be strong for Danny.

Don't think of what might happen.

Take it one day at a time. Focus on the time you have with her.

DANNY

My phone begins to vibrate like crazy, and before I can reach for it, Ryker grabs it away, saying, "I'll reply to the messages."

He looks much calmer than I feel, and when our eyes meet, a smile curves his lips. It blinds me because here I am surrounded by grief, and his light shines through the dark.

Ryker holds his hand out to me, and I instantly reach for it. He pulls me to his side, then says, "As much as this hurts, we have to face it and power through it. Today, this minute is all that matters."

Dad begins to nod as he sucks in a deep breath. "You're right. One day at a time." He pulls me into a hug, and for a moment, I have to let go of Ryker. "We're going to fight this thing head-on."

Uncle Rhett lets out a breath. "Whatever you need, princess, just say the word, and I'll make it happen."

I pull back from Dad then let out a chuckle. "Just treat me normal."

"Done," Uncle Rhett states.

"I need to tell Dash," Christopher says.

I force a smile to my lips. "Try not to worry about me. You'll have to run Indie Ink while I'm getting better."

"I'll take over for you until you can return," Dad says.

"I'm going to have to talk to my dad and Mr. Cutler so they can hold the fort for me while I'm with Danny," Ryker says, immediately taking out his phone to make the calls.

"Let's go pack," Mom tells Dad before glancing my way. "We'll meet you at the plane."

"Okay." I keep the smile around my lips as everyone starts to leave, then Tristan turns to me. There's an aching expression on his face, and it has me saying, "I'm going to be fine. You need to get back to Hana."

He nods then comes to give me a hug before he leaves the room.

When it's just Ryker and me, I sink down on the couch. The second he's done with the calls, he walks to the bedroom. I get up and follow after him.

He pulls our bags out, and it has me moving forward to help him pack.

"I need to update my will," I whisper as I place the dress I wore yesterday in the bag.

Ryker pauses to look at me. "We did one for you last year."

"Yeah, but there's something I want to change," I say.

He turns toward me, the shirt in his hands forgotten. "What?"

"My shares in Indie Ink."

"If I remember correctly, they're divided between Christopher and Tristan," he says.

"Yeah, but with Tristan leaving Indie Ink, I want to name a new beneficiary for his half of the shares." Taking a deep breath, I push through, "You."

Ryker shakes his head hard. "I can't do that."

"As my attorney, you have to. It's my will," I argue.

"No, I mean I can't set it up, not if I'm a beneficiary. Mr. Cutler will have to set it up. It has to be a third party, or it can be contested in court."

It hits hard how calm he is, and it has me asking, "What are you doing? Why are you like this?"

God, is he starting to withdraw from me?

Ryker drops the shirt on the bed then comes toward me. When he takes hold of my shoulders, I begin to tremble.

I don't think I can handle losing him.

"I'm trying to keep calm," he explains. "We're looking at eight months of intense treatment, Danny. It's going to take everything you have in you, so I'm just trying to keep my shit together so I can be strong for you. Okay?"

I begin to nod. "So, you're not pulling away from me?" I ask, needing to know.

"Fuck no," he exclaims, then he takes a deep breath. "I told you I'm not letting you go. I meant it." His eyes jump over my face before they lock on mine. "All I'm asking is that Mr. Cutler deals with it because I can't. Not legally." He shakes his head, and for a moment, the ache bleeds into his eyes.

Wrapping my arms around his neck, I pull him to me. "Okay. I understand. I'll ask Mr. Cutler."

"Thanks. I can do everything else for you, but not that," Ryker murmurs as he folds his arms around me.

I nod against him, then he pulls back. He pauses then says, "I want you to move in today. With me."

I freeze, my eyes widening. "But I'm going to the hospital tomorrow. What's the use?"

"Everything will be ready for when you can come home. I want that home to be my place."

"But... but," I begin to stammer, surprised by his request. "What about my place?"

"We can talk about your place once you're better," Ryker states, then he drops another bomb on me, "I also want us to get engaged before the surgery."

"What?" I gasp.

Ryker's eyes lock on mine with such intensity, I feel it in my bones. "I need some control, Danny. I need to have a say in the choices that are made when you're unable to make them yourself."

E.g., if I end up on life support.

The realization hits me like a ten-ton truck, and I have to sit down on the bed because my legs can't keep me up anymore. "God," I whisper, as the reality of what Ryker has to face sinks in. "I never thought about that."

Ryker crouches in front of me, a pleading expression tightening his features, "And I don't want you to. Let me carry that load. Just give me the power to have a say in your life."

And death.

This is so hard. It's too hard to deal with.

"Do you trust me?" Ryker asks, his voice hoarse with emotion.

"Of course."

"I love you more than anything, Danny. I won't make a decision that's not in your best interest. I promise. I just need to be able to legally fight for you. Give me the power to keep you alive."

I begin to nod, then say, "But getting engaged won't give you a legal foothold."

"I know," he breathes. "But it will help. You also have to decide whether you'll complete a power of attorney and a medical directive naming me as the decision-maker. Those are really the only two documents besides getting married that will give me the right to make decisions for you."

"Can you set up a power of attorney so quickly?" I ask.

Ryker nods. "As soon as we get home."

My eyes lock with his.

I trust Ryker with my life. I would want a say if the roles were reversed.

I'd marry him right now.

I let out a dry chuckle that turns to sob. "How do you feel about marrying a dying woman?"

His features tighten with raw pain. "Don't say things like that." Ryker moves into a kneeling position, pressing his forehead to my knees.

Bringing my hand to his hair, I pull my fingers through the thick strands. "I'm sorry."

When he lifts his head, looking up at me, my palm brushes over his jaw.

"I didn't want to marry you this way," he whispers. "But it's either that or I set up the documents."

"Okay," I breathe. "Let's think for a moment."

Ryker gets up and comes to sit next to me.

"It would be faster to set up the paperwork than getting a marriage license," he says.

"Also true," I murmur. "Get it all drawn up then." Climbing to my feet, I turn to look at him. "I'll give you power of attorney."

Riker rises to his full length and wraps his arms around me. "Thank you. I know it's a lot to deal with, but I promise I'll take good care of you."

I nod, then a weak smile forms around my lips. "So, I'm moving in with you?"

His lips curve up. "Yes. Let's finish here so we can get home. We still have a lot to do." Ryker presses a tender kiss to my mouth then stares deep into my eyes. "Thank you for trusting me."

"With my life?" I whisper, feeling overly emotional. "Always."

Chapter 19

DANNY

We've managed to move my clothes and some of my personal belongings over to Ryker's house. He was driving everything up and down to his house, while I took care of packing it all.

I've just finished rearranging the closet to make space for my clothes and walk to the living room where Ryker is working on a power of attorney.

As I sit down next to him, he scrolls to the top of the page. "Read over it."

I read over the words, then ask, "Do I sign now?"

He shakes his head. "Tomorrow in front of Dr. Friedman. I want him to be a witness, so it can't be contested."

"Okay." I lean back against the couch while my mind goes to the surgery. Suddenly it dawns on me they'll probably shave half my hair off, and it has me darting upright again. "Oh God."

"What?" Ryker startles. "Headache? What? Are you okay?" His eyes dart over me with panic.

"They're going to shave half my hair off for the surgery. The radiation and chemo will probably make me lose whatever's left."

Ryker tilts his head as understanding dawns on his face. "I'm sorry, babe."

Getting up, I rush to the bathroom in Ryker's room and stare at myself in the mirror. Ryker comes in, and lifting his hand, he brushes his palm over my hair. "It will grow back, Danny."

I nod as I swallow hard. "I know, but it doesn't make it any easier." Turning my gaze to his, I ask, "Do you have scissors?"

He begins to frown. "You want to cut it yourself?"

"Rather that than lose it strand by strand." Letting out a sigh, I add, "It gives me some control back."

Ryker nods, and then he walks into the bedroom. He comes back with a chair, a clipper set, and scissors. His eyes lock on mine. "Can I do it?"

We stare at each other for a moment, and then I nod, sitting down on the chair.

Ryker moves in behind me, then he asks, "Where's the incision for the biopsy they did?"

Lifting my hand, I softly press against the still tender spot.

Ryker moves my hair, and then he stills. "I wish you had told me sooner and not gone through that on your own."

"I didn't want to worry you in case it was nothing."

"You going to the hospital alone is not nothing, Danny," he grumbles. He brushes his hand over my hair, and then I feel him pressing a kiss to it. "Are you ready?"

I nod because I can't bring myself to say yes.

Ryker's fingers brush against my neck as he gathers my hair.

I close my eyes and fist my hands, and then I hear the scissors crunch. My face distorts as the tears threaten to fall, but I bite them back as my hair begins to drop to the floor.

After a couple of minutes, Ryker says, "Damn, you look sexy with short hair."

I let out a sputter, which was meant to be a chuckle.

He presses another kiss to what's left of my hair, and then he sets the scissors down and reaches for the clippers. "You're going to look badass like you're joining the army. Kinda fitting for your kick-ass personality."

God, I love this man so much. Even in the darkest time, he tries to make me feel better.

The clippers begin to buzz, and then I feel Ryker's hand on my head. He catches the remaining strands, so they don't fall on my lap.

My body begins to shiver, and when the buzzing ends, I can't bring myself to open my eyes.

Ryker presses another kiss to my head, and then he murmurs, "I love you, Danny."

I nod as I stand up, and opening my eyes, I try not to look at the floor or the mirror. I try and fail miserably. The moment I see the hair on the floor, a sob bursts from me. Ryker yanks the chair out of the way and grabs me to his chest.

"You're still the most beautiful woman on the face of this planet," he says as he begins to press kisses all over my face and head.

I gasp against his chest and try so hard to rein in my tears. This is only the beginning. I can't lose my shit over my hair when I'm fighting for my life.

The thought helps calm me down, and when I look up at Ryker, I even manage to smile. "So, what do you think? Does the look work for me?"

His lips curve up, and there's so much love in his gaze as he says, "Sexy as fuck."

I stare into Ryker's eyes as the realization hits me just how strong he is. How loyal he is. How much he loves me.

Lifting my hand to his jaw, I lift myself on my toes and press a tender kiss to his mouth. When I pull back, I whisper, "You're an amazing man, Ryker. How lucky am I to have you? God... so lucky."

The doorbell rings, and it has Ryker saying, "It's probably my folks. I asked my mom to pick something up for me."

While Ryker goes to open the door, I walk to the closet and dig for a beanie. I pull it on then walk back to the bathroom so I can clean up all the hair. Crouching, I reach for a bundle of strands. I rub them between my thumb and pointer finger, the urge to cry forming a lump in my throat.

"Hey, Danny," I hear Aunt Mia say.

I get up and swallow hard before I turn to face her. "Hey."

"Let me clean that up." My lips part to decline the offer, but then she gives me a compassionate smile. "You shouldn't have to deal with this as well. Let me help. Okay?"

Nodding, I move to the side, still clutching the strands I picked up.

Aunt Mia leaves to get a bag, and coming back, she quickly cleans the floor. Turning to me, she gestures to my hand. "Let me have that, sweetheart."

I glance down and see I have a tight grip on the strands. My hand trembles as I drop it in the bag.

Aunt Mia places the bag on the floor, and then she pulls me into a hug. I grab hold of her as my body begins to shiver.

"It's okay not to be okay right now. You have a lot of people who are here for you. Me, for one."

I nod against her shoulder, and knowing she's helped many people... cross over, I admit, "I'm scared, Aunt Mia. I'm scared of dying."

Aunt Mia pulls back, and her eyes lock with mine. "I know, sweetheart. Try not to let the fear eat you up inside. You're still here. You have a fighting chance. Focus on the now, on today."

Needing to know, I ask, "What do you think happens when we die?"

"In most cases, you're at peace during the final stage. It's always given me hope. It's as if the person already has a glimpse of the other side. That's what I think waits after we pass on. Peace."

Her words calm me enough that my breathing evens out and the shivering subsides. "Thank you. I needed to hear that."

"Whenever you need to talk about it, I'm here."

I nod.

"I've brought a pot roast. Let's go eat."

My lips curve up. "You make the best pot roast."

RYKER

Mom handed me the engagement ring before she went to check on Danny.

Sitting down with Dad, I stare at the diamond ring.

This is not how I wanted to do it.

I wanted to take Danny back to Cape Town, to the guesthouse where we made love for the first time.

"How are you holding up?" Dad asks.

I shake my head. "How am I supposed to process this, Dad?" A breath shudders through my chest, and I close my eyes to keep the tears back. "How?"

"Don't try to make sense of it, son. Just take it one day at a time." The doorbell rings again, and it has me frowning. Then Dad says, "It's your uncles." Dad gets up to open for them.

I rise to my feet when Uncle Carter comes in, followed by Uncle Jaxson, Uncle Marcus, and Uncle Rhett. Including Dad, the five men have always been best friends.

I shake their hands, but Uncle Carter pulls me in for a hug, and then he murmurs, "Thank you, Ryker."

He doesn't have to explain what the thanks is for.

While I have his attention, I say, "I'm asking Danny to marry me. I just wanted you to know."

He pulls back, and our eyes meet. I watch as emotion washes over his face and his eyes mist, then he swallows it down and nods.

"We can just relax in the living room," I hear Mom say, and it has all the men turning to where she's coming down the stairs with Danny.

I hear Uncle Carter suck in a breath when he sees the beanie and that Danny's hair is gone. I place a hand on his lower back and whisper, "She wanted control over this one thing."

He nods as he swallows hard.

Danny stops at the foot of the stairs, and then her face tightens as she tries to keep the tears back.

Uncle Jaxson is the first to move, and walking to her, he pulls her into a hug. "Hey, princess," my father's twin whispers.

"Uncle Jax," she breathes.

It's heartbreaking as I watch our uncles take turns to hug her, but it's when Uncle Marcus hugs her that Danny loses it. "I know it's hard," he says, having almost died himself from a heart problem. He's the reason Mom started working at a hospice.

Danny clings to him as she whimpers, "I'm scared. How did you face it?"

"I didn't," he admits. Uncle Marcus pulls a little back, and framing her face, he says, "You just face it, Danny. Head on. There's no other way." Pressing a kiss to her forehead, he adds, "I'll be there every step of the way. Don't lose hope. Okay? Miracles happen all the time. Look at me."

Danny nods as she wipes the tears from her cheeks. "Thanks, Uncle Marcus."

Everyone grabs a seat in the living room while Mom plates the food. Luckily, she cooked for a small army, not that I think any of us have an appetite.

I wait until we're all done picking at our food, then I take hold of Danny's hand, turning my body to hers.

I tilt my head as my eyes roam over her face. "Isn't she beautiful?"

Everyone hollers, "hell yeah," and it makes Danny smile.

"I think I was twelve or thirteen, and Danny was driving Tristan and me from school. I remember looking up, and I saw Danny's eyes in the rearview mirror. It was the exact same color as the sky. She looked like an angel."

"That's because she is one," Uncle Rhett grumbles.

"Hush, Rhett," Mom snaps, and it draws a chuckle from me.

Smiling, I look at our uncles, "Then I turned sixteen, and you all know what that means."

"Do I have to hear this part?" Uncle Carter mutters, but a grin tugs at the corners of his mouth.

Taking a deep breath, I lock eyes with Danny. "Needless to say, I fell head-over-heels in love with you."

"Okay, now I get why you and Tristan always had sleepovers at his place," Dad says.

I grin at him. "Of course."

Danny lets out a burst of laughter.

Our eyes meet again, and I continue, "Do you know what sealed the deal for me?"

Danny shakes her head.

"The woman you became. You're so strong, Danny. You never back down from a fight, and I've watched you make one man after the other bend to your will."

"Except for you," she mutters. "Stubborn."

"I was already on my knees, praying you'd see me," I admit.

Danny tightens her fingers around mine.

I open my left hand, and as Danny looks down at the ring on my palm, I say, "Now I'm praying I'll be the only man you see. There's no one I'll love more. You're the one I want to spend every day with. You're the one I want to sleep beside. I want to be the man who comforts you, who supports you, who gets to change your last name."

You can hear a pin drop as I murmur, "Marry me, Danny."

She stares at the ring, swallowing hard a couple of times before she lets out a quivering breath. Then she lifts her gaze to mine as she whispers, "I wish I could offer you the world."

"You are my world."

She lets out a sputter, and then she moves forward, wrapping her arms around my neck. "I love you, Ryker. Only you. With everything I am… until…" She makes a heartbreaking sound that has me tightening my arms around her. "Forever. I'll never stop loving you. No matter what happens."

"Did she say yes?" Uncle Rhett whispers, and it has Danny letting out a burst of laughter as she pulls back.

"That's a hell yes, Uncle Rhett."

I slip the ring on her finger.

I promise it will only be you, Danny. Even if the worst happens and you're taken from me – you will be the only woman I'll ever love.

Chapter 20

DANNY

"It was nice of them to come over," I say while I wait for Ryker to lock up and turn off the lights.

"Yeah," he murmurs. Walking toward me, he takes hold of my left hand and tugs me up the stairs. Once we're in his bedroom, he lifts my hand and looks at the ring on my finger. His thumb brushes over the princess-cut diamond, then his mouth curves up. "You're mine now."

A smile spreads over my face as I say, "Thank you for the beautiful ring. I love it."

Ryker's eyes lift to mine, then he says, "I don't plan on sleeping tonight."

"Yeah?" I take a step closer to him. "What do you plan on doing?"

His gaze drifts over my face. "Loving you."

Only then does it hit me that this might be our last night together where we can make love. Not wanting him to see the heartache on my face, I press close to him, resting my cheek against his chest.

Ryker wraps an arm around me, and then he tugs the beanie off my head. My eyes drift closed when his lips brush over my head. "I just want to love you, Danny. I don't want to think of tomorrow or the day after. I want to spend the next eight hours loving every inch of you."

I nod against his chest. My voice is hoarse as I whisper, "I want the same thing."

Ryker moves his hands to my cheeks, and nudging my face up, his eyes find mine. I take in his warm brown irises, his handsome features, the sexy curve of his lips.

He lowers his head until I feel his breath skimming over my mouth. I lift my hands to his jaw, and then his lips tug at mine. It instantly makes my abdomen tighten. Ryker tilts his head, his eyes on mine, and then his mouth claims mine.

The kiss is different than any kiss I've had before. It's poignant, profound, and powerful. I focus wholly on the feel of his lips and his tongue brushing hard strokes against mine.

I drink in the feel of his stubble beneath my palms.

I breathe in his scent.

Ryker presses his body to mine, and lifting me with one arm to him, he moves me back to the bed. I memorize the strength of his body.

He lays me down, and for the longest moment, he just kisses me. By the time his mouth frees mine, I'm breathless.

Sitting up, I pull off my sweater, and it has Ryker climbing off the bed. My eyes are glued to him as he strips out of his clothes. His strong fingers undoing the buttons before his chest is revealed. His hands pushing down his chinos and boxers, and when he's naked, my gaze drifts over his body – muscular, healthy, and oh so hot.

I kick my jeans off, and then Ryker crawls onto the bed, helping me get out of my underwear. He lies down beside me, and it has me turning onto my side to face him.

We stare at each other, losing track of time as we love each other.

Ryker places his hand on my hip, and then his palm brushes up the curve of my body. His eyes drop to where he's touching me as if he's trying to imprint the memory in his mind.

"So fucking beautiful," he whispers as he pulls me closer until our bodies are pressed against each other. Lowering his head, he fuses our mouths together, and then he pushes me onto my back, covering me with every inch of him.

Our hands explore every stretch of skin while our tongues dance to the epic song of our love.

This is the moment I'll keep returning to when things get hard. This is what I'll remember when I exhale my last breath.

Ryker, the man of my dreams, loving me.

RYKER

Every time panic begins to build in my chest, I force it down and focus on Danny.

This might be the last time I get to make love to her. The thought tightens the merciless grip around my heart. My touch grows harder, desperate to keep her with me.

I can't lose you, Danny. I can't. I won't survive. You're the air I breathe.

I position myself at her entrance, and lifting my head, I stare into her sky-blue eyes as I slowly push inside her.

Once I'm buried to the hilt, I focus on how it feels to be one with her. This woman who owns my soul.

My movements are slow as I savor every sensation. Resting my forearms on either side of her head, I just keep staring at her.

It feels as if we're creating our own world where death can't touch us, and God, how I wish it was in my power to make it a reality.

I want to immortalize her.

Danielle Hayes. Unattainable like the stars. Untouchable like the sun.

Did I tempt fate by making her mine?

Was she always supposed to stay just out of my reach?

I can't believe life would be so cruel.

That this is all I'll ever have.

I refuse to believe this is how we end.

Danny's hands brush down the length of my back and down to my ass before she brings them back up to my shoulder blades, drawing me out of my thoughts.

Moving a hand down to her hip, my fingers dig into her skin as I increase the pace. I watch as her lips part, and her eyes cloud over with desire. The sight makes my mouth curve up, and wanting to make her forget… just for a moment… I begin to move fast and hard.

She tips her head back as a gasp drifts over her lips, and then I watch as Danny gets swept away by the pleasure until she comes apart beneath me.

Only then do I allow myself to think of my own need, and latching onto her pulse, I focus on the life beating beneath my lips as I climax.

I push my arms underneath her and clamp her to my chest as I still inside her. Closing my eyes, I feel the heat of her body. I focus on her breaths.

Never in my life have I actually listened to someone breathing. But now it's all I hear, every breath meaning Danny's here with me.

Dread pours through my veins, thinking the day might come where she won't take another breath.

God. No.

I'll do anything. I'll even let her go if it means she gets to live. I'll swap places with her in a heartbeat.

Danny wraps her arms tightly around me, and pressing her mouth to my chest, I feel her breathing change from fast to quivering.

Knowing her thoughts have returned to the cancer, I pull out of her. While Danny goes to the bathroom, I get up, and walking into the closet, I grab a pair of boxers.

I sit down on the edge of the bed, and reaching for the beanie, I pick it up and stare at it until Danny comes out of the bathroom.

My eyes follow her as she walks to the closet to put on a pair of sweatpants and a t-shirt.

When she's done, I rise to my feet, dropping the beanie again.

"There are a couple of things I want to do with you," I say as I reach for her hand.

"Like?"

"Watching a movie. Seeing you in a bikini." I grin at the last idea. "Definitely see you in a bikini."

Danny lets out a burst of laughter. "So, you want me to wear a bikini while we're watching a movie?"

I begin to chuckle. "No." I let go of her hand, and taking a step back from her, I explain, "First we'll watch a movie, pretending we're at my parents' house, and I finally have the guts to hold your hand. Then, I want you to put on a bikini, obviously trying to tempt the shit out of the teenage me."

Danny's smile keeps widening, and then she catches on. "So… your parents went out for dinner, and I'm here to babysit?"

"Yeah," I grin.

She turns around, and as she walks out of the room, she whispers, "Let's do this."

I grab a pair of sweatpants and drag them on before I leave the room.

I find Danny in the kitchen, where she's busy taking microwave popcorn from the cupboard.

Crossing my arms over my chest, I lean against the doorjamb. "Hey, Danny."

"Hey…" she turns around, then tilts her head, "Ryker. All your shirts in the laundry basket?"

I shake my head. "I'm hot."

I'm sure I hear her mumble, "That's for sure."

"Making us popcorn?" I ask.

"Yeah, I figured we can watch a movie." She glances at me from over her shoulder. "Unless you have homework to do?"

"No, all done," I mutter. "I'll pick the movie."

"Nothing adult-rated," she calls after me.

"Yes, ma'am," I chuckle. Reaching for the remote, I drop down on the couch and lift my feet to the coffee table. I turn on the TV, and grinning like an ass, I go to Netflix and select 365 DNI.

I press play, and luckily the title disappears from the screen before Danny comes in with the popcorn. She sets

232

the bowl down between us and looks at the TV as she gets comfortable. "What are we watching?"

"Ah… not sure. Something about a guy kidnapping a girl." I take a handful of popcorn and pop one into my mouth as I press play. Then I tuck the remote under my leg so Danny won't find it.

Roughly eleven minutes into the movie, Danny's eyebrow pops up. "Pretty sure you shouldn't be watching this."

"Sex-Ed," I chuckle.

When a blowjob scene comes on, it has Danny tilting her head. "Daa-yumn, pretty sure he's hitting her tonsils."

I let out a burst of laughter, and it has Danny turning her gaze to me.

Then she goes off-script and turns into my teenage fantasy as she draws her bottom lip between her teeth. "Sex-Ed, right?" she murmurs as she gets up and comes to stand in front of me.

"Yep, I'm failing. Tsk," I murmur.

When she lowers herself to her knees, my heartbeat kicks up.

"Honestly, I've had one blow job, and it almost traumatized me. There were teeth involved," I warn Danny.

She tilts her head as surprise flickers over her face. "For real?"

"Yep, all role-playing aside."

With the playful moment gone, Danny just looks at me, then she asks, "Do you trust me?"

I nod, and it has her pressing herself between my legs. Danny gives me one hell of a seductive look as she presses a kiss to my abs. Then she murmurs, "Relax."

Only because it's Danny do I let out a breath while giving her control. My eyes are locked on her as she begins to remove my sweatpants and boxers, and then her fingers wrap around me, and in seconds I'm hard as fuck.

When Danny lowers her head and her tongue circles the head, air bursts from me.

Christ.

She sucks me into her mouth, and the sight alone is erotic enough to make me lose control. Her lips and tongue work magic on me, and within minutes, I feel my orgasm building. "Gonna come, babe," I warn her.

When she doesn't stop, I begin to reach for her, and it has Danny grabbing hold of my wrist and pinning it to the armrest, and then she sucks hard, and there's no way I can stop myself from coming in her mouth.

"Fuck, Danny," I growl as intense pleasure rips through me. Clenching my jaw, my eyes burn on her as she glances up at me. The instant she lifts her head, licking her fucking lips, I grab hold of her and drag her up my body so I can claim her mouth.

We spend the night worshipping each other, and when the sun breaks through the darkness, my arms tighten around her.

I'm not ready. God, I'm not ready.

Chapter 21

DANNY

Walking into the VIP room in the hospital, I glance around at the red and white décor.

This will be home for a while.

Ryker sets our bags down, then his eyes meet mine. He insisted on packing a bag for himself as well, saying he wasn't leaving my side and that's the end of it.

When a nurse comes into the room, my eyes widen. "Sarah?"

A smile forms around her mouth as she looks at my chart. "Danny. I wondered what your name was."

Moving forward, I hug her and seeing the question on Ryker's face, I explain, "I met Sarah the day I found out."

Her gaze scans over me. "You look much better. How do you feel?"

I nod. "I'm okay. Will you be my nurse?"

"Yes, I just got promoted. Yay me."

I let out a chuckle. "I'm happy for you."

She glances at the chart again, then says, "I need to do a couple of checks. Sit on the bed for me."

I do as she says and wait for her to take my blood pressure and temperature. After she's written it down, she says, "You're scheduled for an MRI at eleven. I'll also have to draw blood." She gives me an evil grin. "Yeah, I get to stick a needle in you."

"Have at it," I chuckle, really glad to see her again.

While Sarah is drawing blood, she glances at Ryker, then she says, "Your boyfriend looks like the silent type."

"Shoot, sorry. This is Ryker, my fiancé," I introduce them quickly.

Ryker just gives her a chin lift. "Hey."

"Yeah, I guess he's the silent type," I joke.

When Sarah is done with everything, she turns to Ryker. "Will it be just the two of us taking care of Danny?"

"Her family will be here shortly," he answers.

Sarah shakes her head. "Yeah, but I'm guessing you'll be staying here twenty-four-seven?"

"Oh… yeah," Ryker answers.

"Okay, let me show you a couple of things." Sarah goes through a list of things, the panic button, how the bed works, how the fold-out bed works for when Ryker wants to use it.

237

When she's done, she smiles at both of us. "Get comfortable. I'm just going to take the bloodwork to the lab."

After Sarah leaves the room, Ryker comes to sit next to me on the bed. "She looks like a nice person."

"She is. She comforted me without knowing anything about the cancer or who I was. It felt like an angel stepped into my hell to pull me back up," I admit.

Ryker takes a deep breath as he gets up again. "Still wish you told me sooner." He walks to my bag and opening it, he takes out a pair of sweatpants and a t-shirt. "Get changed so you can get comfortable."

Rising to my feet, I take the clothes from him. I stand on my toes and press a kiss to his mouth. "Thank you for being here now."

His lips curve up. "There's nowhere else I'd rather be."

I slip into the bathroom to change, and while taking off my clothes, I hear Mom's voice. "Where's Danny?"

"Changing," Ryker answers. "What's that?"

"A couple of things to make this room feel like home."

"Let me help you."

"Carter told me you and Danny got engaged last night." I hear the hurt tone in her voice and hurry.

"Yes," Ryker answers. "I'll take good care of her."

When I step back into the room, a smile spreads over my face when I see all the framed photos of my family on the window sill. My favorite teddy from when I was little rests on the bed.

"Mom, you didn't have to," I chuckle.

"I think it will help keep your spirits up," she says as she comes to hug me.

"Thank you." I pull back and lock eyes with her. "I'm sorry I didn't call last night. Things were a little overwhelming."

Mom waves a hand. "Don't worry about it. Let me see the ring."

Mom fawns over the engagement ring, and then I sit down on the bed. Her gaze drifts over the beanie I'm wearing, but she doesn't say anything about my hair being gone.

I glance at the photos again, then looking at Ryker, I say, "I don't have a photo of you."

He takes his phone out and comes to sit next to me. Wrapping his arm around my shoulders, he pulls me against his side, and then we smile.

"Send it to me, and I'll get it developed and framed," Mom offers.

"That would be great," Ryker replies as he forwards it to her phone.

Uncle Logan comes into the room with an envelope, and after greeting us, he hands it to Ryker.

"I wish I could stay, but I need to get back to the office," Uncle Logan says to me.

"Of course. I understand."

"Your Dad said to tell you he'll be here in thirty minutes. He's just organizing things at Indie Ink."

"Thanks." I smile as he leaves, then I glance at Ryker. He's reading over the documents and knowing what they are, my gaze turns to Mom. I don't want her to find out when Dr. Friedman gets here.

"Mom, come sit." I pat the bed, and when she's seated next to me, I say, "I'm giving Ryker power of attorney." Mom begins to frown, and it has me explaining, "It's so he can make medical decisions on my behalf, should I not be able to."

Mom's eyes widen, and then they dart to Ryker before coming back to me. "I understand the two of you are in love, but that's huge, Danny."

I shake my head. "We're not in love, Mom. We love each other. I would want the same power if the roles were reversed. As my fiancé, he won't have a say, and I can't

240

leave him in such a vulnerable position. I feel Ryker should have a say… when… the end comes."

Mom closes her eyes as pain tightens her features. Then she begins to shake her head. "That's not going to happen."

I swallow hard as I reach for her hand. "Mom, we both know there's a possibility the treatment won't work."

"Still," she gasps, fighting to keep the tears back. "Do we have to talk about this now?"

"We do. I'm going for surgery tomorrow. There's no time. We have to face the facts."

God, this is hard. It's near impossible having to be the strong one when I'm the one dying.

There's a hard blow to my gut as my grim reality washes over me again. Ryker has managed to make me forget for a while… a precious short time.

I turn my gaze to Ryker, and it has him getting up and walking to me. He wraps his arm around me, then says, "Aunt Della. Danny is everything to me."

"She's everything to me, as well," Mom cries as she gets up. "God, she's my daughter."

Just then, Dad comes into the room, and I know things are going to go bad really fast.

RYKER

Uncle Carter takes hold of Aunt Della, then he asks, "What's going on."

Aunt Della answers, her voice tight, "Danny's giving Ryker power of attorney so he can make medical decisions on her behalf."

Uncle Carter's eyes snap to mine, then to Danny. "Seriously? Why would you do that, Danny?"

"Because Ryker is my other half," Danny answers.

"You just got engaged. You haven't even been dating that long," Uncle Carter argues.

"It doesn't change the fact that we love each other. I'm doing this with or without your approval," Danny says, her voice starting to quiver.

Hearing how close to tears Danny is, I jump in. "I understand she's your daughter. I'm not going to just make random decisions. I'll discuss them with you."

"You'll still have the power to take her off life support or to reject any further treatment that could've made a difference," Aunt Della cries.

Uncle Carter's face turns to granite, and I know I'm in for the fight of my life.

"Which is something I will never do," I state, my own voice tense.

Danny lets out a sob, and it has me wrapping both my arms around her.

Locking eyes with Uncle Carter, I say, "Danny's my entire life. I need a say in what happens to her. I won't go against your wishes unless it's to terminate life support. I'll never agree to that."

Uncle Carter's eyes drop to Danny. "Is this really what you want, Danny?"

She nods against my abs. "It is. This isn't... about who... I love... or trust most. Like I told Mom... if the roles were reversed... I'd want a say in what happens... to Ryker. This is a decision... we made together."

Uncle Carter shakes his head, then his eyes lock on mine. "You do not make a single decision without me."

"I won't," I assure him.

I can see they're unhappy about this, but I won't back down. Danny's my entire life. If I lose her and it was in my power to save her... that will never happen.

Not long after the argument, Dr. Friedman comes into the room. He greets Uncle Carter and Aunt Della, then he shakes my hand.

He pretty much repeats what he said over the phone yesterday, but seeing the positive light in his eyes gives me hope.

His eyes rest on Danny with a compassionate smile softening his features. "Thank you for trusting my team and me."

Danny nods, even managing to smile back at him. "Thank you... for allowing me... to take part in the trial."

Dr. Friedman tilts his head, then he moves closer to Danny. "How was the wedding?"

"It was... perfect."

Seeing the worry on his face, I ask, "What's wrong?"

"Danny's speech is stilted. Does it happen often?"

I shake my head. "It's only happened a couple of times. Mostly when she's upset."

Dr. Friedman nods, but then Uncle Carter asks, "Is it a bad sign?"

Dr. Friedman only says, "It's a symptom." His eyes lock with Danny's. "It should return to normal once we've done the surgery."

Taking a deep breath, I pick up the two documents and hold them out to Dr. Friedman. "We need to sign this in your presence, as well as have another witness to state Danny was sound of mind when she made this decision."

Dr. Friedman takes the documents from me, and then he reads them. "A medical directive and power of attorney." His gaze snaps to Danny. "Do you know what this means?"

Danny nods. "Ryker will have the power to make any medical decisions on my behalf."

"Including the refusal of treatment," Dr. Friedman states. He moves closer to Danny. "The court views this as a living will of sorts. You can make your own choices now. We can list them in the document."

We spent the next hour adding Danny's wishes to documents, and then we finally get to sign them.

With the added wishes from Danny, I can see Uncle Carter and Aunt Della feel much better about everything, and it eases the tension in the air.

Chapter 22

DANNY

The only sound in the room comes from the TV that's on a music channel. My gaze jumps from Mom to Dad to Ryker, who are all deep in thought.

We've discussed everything there is to discuss. All the tests have been done. Now we wait.

I let out a sigh. It's going to be a long night, by the looks of things.

The door opens, and when I see Uncle Rhett, a smile instantly tugs at my lips.

He glances at everyone then lifts his eyebrows. "Looks like I came just in time," he grumbles as he walks to me. He presses a kiss to my forehead then holds out a DVD to me. "For old time's sake."

Frozen.

Emotion washes over me. "Aww... Uncle Ledge." I grin at him. "Let's do this."

He puts in the DVD then comes to sit on the bed with me. I snuggle against my godfather's side, and a soft smile forms on my face as *Frozen* begins.

I reach for his shirt and begin to rub the fabric between my forefinger and thumb as we watch our movie for the millionth time.

When it nears our favorite scene, I slap Uncle Rhett against his arm as I sit up. "Get ready, Uncle Ledge."

He straightens up as the song starts, and we begin to sing along. When it gets to the chorus, we're belting the lyrics at the top of our voices. "Let it go. Let it go. Can't hold it back anymore!"

By the time the song ends, we're both breathless as we begin to laugh.

Just then, Christopher and Dash come into the room, followed by Tristan and Hana.

"I thought I heard *Frozen*," Christopher chuckles.

After everyone has said hello, Ryker asks, "Why do you call Uncle Rhett Uncle Ledge?"

"Cause I'm a fucking legend," Uncle Rhett answers.

Letting out a chuckle, I explain, "I couldn't say legend when I was little, so I abbreviated it to ledge."

"It was at your princess party for your fourth birthday," Dad adds, then he begins to chuckle. "Rhett dressed up as a jester, bells and all."

"I rocked that shit," Uncle Rhett laughs.

"That will be a hundred dollars," Aunt Jamie says as she comes into the room with Uncle Julian, her husband.

"Highway robbery," Uncle Rhett grumbles as he takes cash from his wallet, but there's a huge smile on his face.

Aunt Jamie swipes the money from his hand, then she looks at me. "Want to walk with me to get some coffee? Your uncle's treat."

Uncle Rhett pauses the movie. "We can watch the rest later." Which means he's staying for a while. The thought that I'll have my family with me fills my heart with warmth.

I get up off the bed and slip on my shoes.

Before I leave with Aunt Jamie and Mom, I give Uncle Julian a hug. "Thanks for being here."

"Of course." His eyes scan over my face. "Let me know if you need anything. Okay?"

I nod and then go to press a kiss to Ryker's lips before I leave the room. I hook my arm through Aunt Jamie's then say, "Thanks for coming. The surgery is at seven, so I can't have coffee."

"Shoot." Aunt Jamie comes to a sudden stop.

Tugging at her arm, I say, "But you can have some. Come on. The walk will do me good."

I reach for Mom's hand, and her fingers instantly clamp around mine.

"Remember when it was just the three of us?" I ask

"Yeah." A nostalgic smile spreads over Aunt Jamie's face.

"It was hard times, but we had fun," Mom murmurs. "God, that pink phase you went through. You drove us insane."

I let out a chuckle, remembering that was around the time Dad found us and our lives changed forever.

RYKER

The instant Danny leaves, it feels like a shroud of death descends over the room. It has me standing up and shaking my head, I say, "We've all taken this hard, but we need to get our shit together. For Danny. This is going to be hard enough on her as is. We need to cheer her up and remind

249

her what she's fighting for." I lock eyes with Uncle Rhett. "Like watching Frozen with her. We need to come up with things like that."

"I have a whole collection of DVDs I can watch with her," Uncle Rhett says.

"Tristan and I can play board games with her," Christopher mentions.

"I'll keep her up to date with what's happening at work," Uncle Carter mutters.

Everyone begins to brainstorm, and it lifts the mood in the room a little. I pull my phone out and send a text to the group chat telling them the same thing.

Danny comes back with Aunt Jamie and Aunt Della, and they hand out the coffees they got.

When the room grows quiet, I say, "Let's watch the rest of Frozen, Uncle Rhett."

He presses play, and I watch as Danny grins at the funny scenes. She lip-syncs along to every song. When the movie comes to an end, Christopher and Dash get up to leave, and not soon after, Tristan and Hana follow.

Aunt Jamie and Uncle Julian stay for a while before they call it a night as well. Danny looks at her parents and Uncle Rhett. "You should go home and get some rest."

"Yeah," Uncle Carter says as he gets up. He gives Danny a tight hug. "I'll see you first thing tomorrow."

Aunt Della and Uncle Rhett hug Danny, and then they leave. I grab a pair of sweatpants and a t-shirt from my bag, then say, "I'm just going to shower quickly."

Danny lies back on the bed, her eyes following me into the ensuite bathroom.

I rush through my routine, and when I'm done, Danny pats the space beside her on the bed. "Lie with me."

We have to maneuver ourselves until she's draped half over me and it has us grinning. "Hey, beautiful," I murmur, my gaze locking with hers.

"Hey, handsome." She lifts herself and presses a kiss to my mouth, then we stare at each other for a little while before I pull her closer for another kiss.

Danny ducks her head under my chin, and it has me pulling the beanie off her. I brush my hand over the buzzcut she has and then press my mouth to her head.

Wanting to lift her spirits, I say, "When you're done with treatment, I was thinking we can visit Cape Town again."

"Yeah," she chuckles. "We can do the wine route again."

I let out a burst of laughter. "I'll just skip all the wine. That hangover sucked ass."

Danny glances up at me. "Why didn't you tell me you had feelings for me?"

I shift her a little, so we're comfortable while looking at each other. "I thought you only saw me as Tristan's friend."

"Yeah, his hot friend," she teases me.

"At least, I flirted with you," I mention. "You gave me zero indication you were interested."

Danny shrugs. "The age gap. You being Tristan's friend. You know."

"Still, how did you hide your feelings so well?"

She grins at me. "Trust me, it was torture. You didn't make it easy at all."

"At least I know how to get you to let your guard down," I joke.

"How?"

"Wine. Lots of wine."

Danny lets out a soft burst of laughter, and then she snuggles closer to me. "To think I almost missed my chance of having this with you."

I tighten my arms around her.

Five weeks.

God, don't let that be all we get.

252

"Love you, Danny," I murmur.

"Love you," she whispers, and then silence falls around us. It doesn't take long for Danny to fall asleep.

I'm torn between staying awake, so I won't miss a second with her and getting rest after the rough weekend we had.

I press another soft kiss to her head then close my eyes, knowing I'll need the rest for what's to come.

Chapter 23

DANNY

I wake up in the same position I fell asleep in, with Ryker's arms wrapped around me.

When he tightens his hold on me, I whisper, "I woke up on the plane, and the second I realized you were holding me, I pretended to be asleep so I could savor the feel of your arms around me."

He lets out a deep chuckle. "I was lying on my side, just staring at you, and then you snuggled up to me. God, it felt like heaven's gates were opening to me."

"Even in my sleep, I gravitate to you," I whisper. Knowing my surgery is in a couple of hours, I swallow hard as emotion wells in my chest. "Maybe it will be the same if the worst happens. I'll find a way to gravitate to you."

Ryker's arms tighten even more around me. His body begins to shake but only for a minute before he reins it in again. "Just focus on fighting for us, Danny. Don't think about anything else. Just keep fighting."

I nod against his chest, and taking a deep breath, I say, "The past five weeks have been a dream come true. Thank you for loving me, Ryker." Slowly, I let out a quivering breath while my eyes tear up. "You're everything I've wanted in this life."

The shaking returns to his body, and it makes tears sneak from my eyes. Ryker moves his hands to my face and tilts my head back. When our eyes meet, and I see the heartache in his, a sob flutters over my lips.

"Loving you is both the easiest and hardest thing I've ever had to do. Easy because you're the air I breathe." I swallow, and his voice becomes hoarse as he continues, "And hardest because I can't let go of you. Ever. You're my life, Danny. Without you, I have nothing to live for."

Ryker's been so strong since I told him, it was easy to forget what my death would do to him.

Not wanting him to mourn me for the rest of his life, I say, "If I die, I want you to live for both of us. I want you to love again, to be happy. To have a family of your own."

Ryker clenches his jaw, and shaking his head, he pulls me back to his chest. "I'll do anything for you, Danny. But not that. You're it for me. You're the only woman I'll ever love, and no other will compare to you. Don't bring it up again."

Hopefully, time will change his mind, but knowing the pain is too new, too raw and incessant, I let the subject go.

I snuggle closer to him, then whisper, "I love you, Ryker West. You're the prince I always wanted."

He presses a kiss to my head. "You've always been my princess."

Our time alone comes to an end as Sarah comes into the room. "Morning." Her eyebrows lift as Ryker sits up. "Did I interrupt something?"

I let out a burst of laughter. "No, we just woke up."

"Did you get a good night's rest?" Sarah asks.

"Actually, I did."

As Sarah takes my temperature and blood pressure, she says, "That's good to hear." She looks at Ryker. "I'll sit with Danny if you want to get some coffee."

He clears his throat, then murmurs, "Thanks." Ryker grabs a change of clothes and heads into the bathroom.

Then Sarah pulls a chair closer. "Tell me something about yourself."

"Like?" I ask as I glance at her.

"Anything. What do you want me to know?"

I think for a second, then say, "Everybody at work thinks I'm this big powerhouse, but I'm actually a pushover."

Just then, Ryker comes out of the bathroom, looking hot in his jeans and button-up shirt. "She's lying, Sarah. She rules Indie Ink with an iron fist. I should know. She's threatened to demote me a couple of times."

Sarah lets out a chuckle. "Now the truth comes out."

Ryker comes to press a kiss on my head then he leaves to get some coffee.

"How long have you been a couple?" Sarah asks.

"Five weeks."

My answer has her eyebrows shooting up. "Wow, you guys move fast."

Laughing, I explain, "Our families are close friends, so I've known him all my life."

"Ahh… I see."

"We went on a business trip to Africa, and one thing led to another, and now here we are," I explain.

A soft smile spreads over Sarah's face. "I can see he loves you a lot."

"Yeah?"

She nods, then she asks, "Besides work, tell me something else about you."

I shrug. "Before Ryker and I coupled up, there was only work."

"So, you're a work-a-holic," she states dryly.

"Pretty much."

"You're going to have to make some changes. You know that, right?" Sarah asks.

I nod. "If I survive, I'm going to spend more time living and less time working."

"That's good to hear."

But most of my time I'll spend loving Ryker and my family. I'll never take time for granted again.

RYKER

I'm sitting on the side of Danny's bed, my fingers linked with hers. I keep staring at the engagement ring, knowing she'll have to take it off in the next couple of minutes.

My thumb brushes over her finger, and then I pull the ring off. Lifting Danny's hand, I press a kiss to the empty spot, then I smile at her.

Suddenly Miss Sebastian rushes into the room. "Mother of fashion, traffic was a nightmare. I sounded like a drunken sailor all the way here. Road rage is a real thing." She comes to hug Danny, then wraps her arm around my shoulders. Looking at Danny, she asks, "How are you feeling, my angel-girl?"

"Nervous," Danny admits. "But okay." She shrugs. "It is what it is."

Miss Sebastian reaches over and takes hold of Danny's hand. "Don't downplay it for the sake of your family."

Danny shakes her head. "It's for my sake, or I'll go insane."

Instantly overwhelming frustration tightens my chest.

I hate this. God, I hate what Danny has to go through.

"I'll be here after the surgery to help with your recovery. Okay?" Miss Sebastian says.

"Thanks, Mamma G." Danny tries to smile, but with the surgery happening in the next twenty minutes, none of us can smile.

When Sarah and another nurse come into the room, I get up from the bed, grabbing hold of Danny's hand.

God. I'm not ready for this.

"Time to go, Danny," Sarah says.

Danny pulls her hand from mine and goes to hug her parents and brothers.

Keep your shit together, Ryker. Just until she leaves. Don't let her see your fear.

When Danny turns to me, I somehow manage to smile at her. She comes to stand in front of me, and I lift my hand to her head, brushing my palm over the right side. "I'll see you in a couple of hours. Okay?"

Danny nods as she swallows hard.

"I love you, Daniele Hayes."

She lets out a slow quivering breath, then whispers, "I love you, Ryker. So much."

There are a million words I still want to say, but none of them can form on my lips. Leaning down, I press a tender kiss to her trembling lips, and then I murmur, "You're a fighter. Don't forget that."

She nods as she begins to pull away. My eyes stay locked on her until she disappears down the hallway.

My chest begins to shudder.

I close my eyes as a wave of despair hits.

I place a hand on the bed as a deep ache bleeds through me, and then it hits.

Danny has cancer.

Danny might die.

And there's nothing I can fucking do.

I suck in a breath of air, but it sounds strangled.

"Ryker," I hear Tristan say.

I feel a hand on my back and know it's Miss Sebastian. Opening my eyes, I try to rein in the devastating pain as I turn my gaze to Tristan's.

The moment our eyes meet, he comes toward me, and then I'm pulled into a hug. "Take a moment to break. She'll need you to be strong when she comes out of surgery."

I grab hold of his back as the shaking in me grows, and then I groan, "I can't lose her."

"None of us can," he whispers, his voice hoarse.

I break in my best friend's arms. "Fuck," I groan, the ache becoming too overwhelming to breathe through.

I feel another hand on my arm, and then I'm pulled into Mom's arms. "I've got you, my baby. Mom's here."

A suffocating sound rumbles through my chest, and it has Mom pulling back. She frames my face and locks her gaze on mine. "Breathe, Ryker."

Nodding, I suck in a painful breath.

"Danny's going to be fine. Okay? The surgery will go well."

I cling to Mom's words and nod again.

"Let's go for a walk. The change of scenery will do you good."

Mom takes hold of my arm, tugging me forward, and somehow my legs move. Miss Sebastian falls in on my other side, linking her fingers with mine.

I feel like a zombie as I let them lead me outside to a garden. We sit down on a wooden bench, and then I rest my elbows on my knees before I cover my mouth with my hands. I stare blankly at the surrounding nature.

After a couple of minutes, I manage to mutter, "How am I supposed to process any of this? Danny's thirty-two. She's so young."

"These things never make any sense," Mom murmurs.

I shake my head. "What if she can't beat it? What then? How... how do I go on without her?"

"You just do, Ryker. It will be hard, but with time –"

"Don't tell me it will get easier. It won't," I snap. "It's always been Danny, Mom. I've always loved her. I won't move on. I won't find someone new. It will only be Danny."

Miss Sebastian places her hand on my back.

"Ryker," Mom murmurs.

My eyes dart to her. "Could you move on if Dad died?"

Mom's features tighten, and she lifts a hand to the back of my neck. "No... no, I wouldn't be able to."

"Then don't expect me to," I mutter. "Danny's my once-in-a-lifetime love. She's my everything. Without her, my life has no meaning."

Mom wraps her arms around me. She doesn't try to offer me any empty words of wisdom. She just holds me as I'm sucked back into the wasteland my life was before I got to hold Danny. Before I got to kiss her. Before I got to make love to her.

That's all that's left without Danny. Nothing but a desert without the hope of seeing a mirage.

I won't survive losing her.

I won't be able to live without her.

If she goes, I go.

Chapter 24

RYKER

I keep sitting outside with Mom and Miss Sebastian, part of me too scared to go back inside.

The helplessness of knowing Danny's life depends on a man I know very little about eats away at me. There's nothing I can do, and it strips me bare of all my strength.

I know I'm not the first person to go through this, but... how am I supposed to just sit with my hands tied while I watch the life drain out of her?

This woman who's so full of life. So vibrant and strong. How am I supposed to...

I can't feel happiness without her smile.

I can't feel love unless I'm looking into her eyes.

I feel weak without her strength.

I let out a slow breath, then suck in a deep one.

"We should go in," Miss Sebastian murmurs. "They'll give updates about the surgery."

Nodding, I force myself to get up. I follow Mom and Miss Sebastian to the waiting room. Seeing the grim expressions on the faces of Danny's family members makes the blow hit again.

I drop down on the nearest chair, and after a couple of minutes, the silence becomes stifling. Getting up again, I step out of the waiting room. I lean back against a wall, crossing my arms over my chest.

Closing my eyes, I focus on my breathing, praying time will pass quickly so I can see Danny again.

But instead, time crawls at a snail's pace.

It intensifies the fear, the despair, the all-consuming deep ache.

God, please let the surgery be successful.

Let the treatment work.

Please. Please. Please, let Danny be one of the few who beats this thing.

Lifting my head, I see Dad, Uncle Jaxson and Uncle Marcus walking toward me. Uncle Marcus pats my shoulder before he heads into the waiting room.

"How are you holding up?" Dad asks, his eyes filled with concern.

Uncle Jaxson comes to stand next to me, assuming the same position as me while muttering, "He's not." He lets out a sigh. "All you can do is push through. It's shitty, I know."

Uncle Jaxson had to face something similar when Uncle Marcus almost died. They've been best friends since forever.

"It's hard," I breathe.

Uncle Jaxson presses his shoulder to mine. "I was sitting in the waiting room while they were operating on Marcus, slowly losing my fucking mind."

I just listen as I lower my eyes to the tiled floor.

"Danny was four or five years old. She came in and walked straight to me. She climbed onto my lap and kissed my cheek, asking me why I looked so sad."

He clears his throat before he continues, "I told her my heart's a little broken, and she placed her tiny hand on my chest, telling me not to cry. Of course, I lost my shit, and I started bawling my eyes out. Know what she did?"

I shake my head, picturing Danny as a little girl.

"She just kept saying it's okay... it's okay. She wrapped her arms around me then said, just don't get snot on me. I began laughing and crying at the same time." He lets out a chuckle. "She even checked her t-shirt to make sure I didn't snot all over her."

My lips curve up.

Uncle Jaxson lets out a sigh. "There are no answers, Ryker. Sometimes life just fucking sucks."

I nod, totally agreeing with him.

My Dad and Uncle Jaxson just stand with me as silence falls around us.

Five hours and nineteen minutes.

That's how long we have to wait before Dr. Friedman walks toward us. His features are tight, and the sight makes my mouth dry with fear. Pins and needles spread over me.

I try to suck in a breath, but it slams into my throat.

God. Please.

My heart begins to speed up, and Dad ducks into the waiting room. "The doctor's here."

I hear movement, and then everyone spills out into the hallway.

Dr. Friedman takes hold of my arm, giving it a squeeze as he looks at Uncle Carter. "The surgery went well. There were no complications. We got it all out. We did what we call a super maximal resection, which means we took out the tumor and then some. I think we managed to get it all. I've given Danny the injections, and I'm hoping it infects whatever cells we might've missed. She's in recovery right now. You'll be able to see her soon, but we will keep her in the ICU for two days. In twenty-four hours, I'll administer the Valtrex treatment to kill the herpes and whatever's left of the tumor."

"So, it went really well?" Uncle Carter asks.

"Much better than I expected. We're off to a good start."

I close my eyes as I take in the fantastic news. It numbs my legs and sliding down against the wall, I crouch as I cover my face with my hands.

Oh God.

I suck in a desperate breath as my body shudders. An arm falls around my shoulders, and without having to look, I know it's Tristan.

I just keep focusing on my breaths until the strength returns to my legs. When I rise to my full height, I turn to Tristan, and we hug. Relief is palpable in the air, knowing Danny just made it through the first stage.

That's my badass girl. Just keep fighting.

Walking into the ICU, it feels like I can finally breathe when my eyes land on Danny.

She has a nasal cannula to assist with breathing, and the buzzcut she had on her right side has been shaved off.

Other than that, she looks much better than I expected, with only a dressing covering the incision.

Leaning down, I press a kiss to her forehead while taking hold of her hand. "You did so well, babe."

When she slowly nods, I pull back, and seeing her eyes open, a broad smile spreads over my face. "Hey, beautiful."

"Hey," she slurs.

"How do you feel?"

When Danny manages to smile, the death grip on my heart lessens.

"Okay… for someone… who just had… brain surgery."

Dr. Friedman lets out a chuckle as he comes closer with Uncle Carter and Aunt Della following behind him. "Look at you talking fifteen minutes after surgery. Quite the fighter."

"Of… course," she chuckles breathlessly.

My God, she's so strong.

Dr. Friedman waits for Uncle Carter and Aunt Della to kiss Danny, then he takes hold of her hand. "Squeeze for me." Danny only manages to stir her fingers, but Dr. Friedman murmurs, "Good. That's very good." He checks her other hand and her legs before he smiles. "You'll feel some muscle weakness, which is normal, and it will pass.

Once we've administered the Valtrex treatment, we'll move you back to your room."

"But... everything... went okay?" Danny asks, her voice sounding stronger.

"Yes, we got it all. The treatment will take care of the rest. It's increased your chances for survival by a lot. I can't give you a number of years, but it's positive. Okay?"

Danny's smile widens. "Thank... you."

"No, thank you, Danny. Thanks for trusting me and for being so brave."

I tighten my hold on her hand, wanting to hug the living shit out of the doctor.

"Get some rest," Dr. Friedman says before he smiles at me.

"Thank you so much," I murmur, wishing there was a way I could express my gratitude.

Every year or even every month he can give us means everything to me. A cure might come along, or a new treatment. Time. We just need more time, and right now, he's given it to us.

"I'll be right back." I go after Dr. Friedman and catch him in the hallway. "Doctor."

He turns around and smiles when he sees me. Holding out my hand to him, he instantly takes it. "Thank you so much for what you've done and what you're still going to do. I can't tell you how much I appreciate it."

A comforting expression settles on his face. "I'm just doing what I'd do for any of my family members. I lost my father to Glioblastoma, so I'm really passionate about it."

"I'm just grateful we have you as Danny's doctor."

He leans in, giving me a quick pat on the back. "Stay strong. Okay? We're going to kick cancer's butt."

I let out a chuckle because doctors were always just... doctors. Looking at the man as he walks away, I'm filled with awe at the miracle he performed today, and it makes me see him in a whole new light.

Rushing back to Danny, I take hold of her hand again, and I can't stop smiling from just seeing her alive.

Right now, she's here. She's still with me.

That's all that matters.

Chapter 25

DANNY

Besides headaches, my speech slurring, and muscle weakness, I feel much better than I thought I would.

I was moved back to my room early this morning, and I'm totally taking that as another win. Dr. Friedman said he wants to wait a week before starting with radiation just so I can get a little stronger.

My parents, Uncle Rhett, and Aunt Jamie went to get us breakfast. Christopher and Tristan also just left to get back to work.

It's just Ryker and me for a precious couple of minutes. I love my family and friends, but it's overwhelming trying to deal with everyone all at once.

I try to tighten my hold on his hand, and it has his eyes snapping to my face, and then a smile tugs at his lips. "You're getting stronger."

"Yeah," I murmur. Taking a deep breath, I say, "Can you do me a favor?"

"Anything." He leans closer, wrapping his other hand around my wrist. He keeps holding onto me as if he's afraid I'll disappear if he lets go.

"Can you talk to everyone? It's overwhelming if they visit in groups."

Ryker nods. "Two at a time?"

I nod, my mouth curving up. "Please."

"I'll take care of it," he says, and leaning over me, he presses a kiss to my lips.

When he starts to pull back, I whisper, "Wait. I want to smell you."

Ryker closes the small distance, and then his lips brush over my jaw and cheek while I take a deep breath of him. Closing my eyes, I focus only on him, and it helps me to relax.

"I love you," I murmur.

Ryker brings one of his hands to the left side of my face, and then he just stares at me. Seeing how much he cares for me… reminds me of what I'm fighting for.

This man.

I need to live for him.

His mouth curves up into the sexy smile I love so much, and it draws a chuckle from me. "God. That smile."

"Only for you, babe," he murmurs.

"I better not catch you smiling like that at anyone else, or it will be you lying in this bed."

Ryker chuckles, and hearing the sound brings unexpected tears to my eyes. It has me whispering, "My favorite sound." I take in his handsome features, then add, "You're my favorite everything."

"You're my favorite too," he grins.

He looks so happy it has me saying, "You look very happy."

"It's because you're kicking this thing's ass, just like I knew you would."

We bask in the win we just had, and then Ryker sends out a message to everyone to only visit two at a time. When he puts his phone away, he mutters, "This room is going to get very busy with everyone wanting to check on you. Let me know whenever you need to rest so I can make sure it's quiet."

My lips curve up again, and I manage to lift my hand to his arm. "I'm so lucky to have you."

Ryker tilts his head, then he murmurs, "I'm the lucky one."

When my cousin, Jase, and Ryker's sister, Mila, come into the room, I smile.

Mila places a cute tiny bear on my lap. "We weren't sure if you were allowed to receive flowers."

"He's perfect. Thank you."

Jase grips hold of my right hand. "How are you holding up?"

I shrug. "I'm doing okay."

Mila looks at my left hand, then she asks, "Aren't you allowed to wear jewelry?"

"Oh shit," Ryker mutters. "With everything that happened, I forgot." He pulls the ring from his breast pocket then comes to slip it back onto my finger.

Mila lifts my hand to look at the ring, then she gives her older brother a teasing grin. "Not bad." Her gaze turns back to me. "I always wanted an older sister."

"Well, I've got the older part covered," I chuckle.

I'm eleven years Mila's senior, but before I can start feeling awkward, Ryker leans over me, pressing a kiss to my left temple.

Jase gives me a playful grin. "Are you ready for some news?"

"Give it to me."

"Mila's agreed to be my PA."

I let out a sputter of laughter, then glance at Mila. "Are you sure that's what you want to do?"

"Someone has to keep him in line," she mutters.

Jase took over as CEO of CRC Holdings, our sister company, and I know his current PA, Stephanie, is retiring soon.

"Just don't let it interfere with your relationship," I warn them.

"We won't," Jase assures me. "We're also planning on getting married at the end of the year."

Not knowing what the future holds for me, my smile dims a little. Glancing at Mila's left hand, I ask, "Where's the ring?"

Mila lets out a chuckle. "We actually just got to talking about getting married, but he hasn't proposed yet."

My eyebrow lifts as I turn my gaze to Jase, and it has him saying, "I'm hoping she'll forget about it so I can actually surprise her."

"Yeah?" Ryker asks. "And how's that working for you?"

Jase shakes his head. "Not in my favor."

We all chuckle then Mila gives my hand a squeeze. "We'll visit again. Keep getting better. Okay?"

Nodding at her, I say, "Thanks for popping in. I appreciate it."

Jase leans closer and presses a kiss to my forehead. "Love you."

I give my cousin a warm smile. "Love you too." I watch as Jase takes hold of Mila's hand, and after they leave the room, I murmur, "I'm happy for them."

"Yeah," Ryker agrees as he sits down again, linking his fingers with mine. He presses a kiss to my ring finger, then just stares at me.

"How do you feel about your sister marrying my cousin?" I ask.

Ryker shrugs. "Jase is a good man. I know he'll take care of her." Then he lets out a chuckle. "You know Dash and Mila both have the twin gene, right?"

A wide smile spreads over my face. "God, I'd pay good money to see Christopher's face if they're expecting twins."

"That makes two of us."

Tilting my head, I say, "That means you have the gene as well."

"Yeah, but I can only pass it on to my daughter."

My smile fades as I murmur, "Your daughter."

"Our daughter," Ryker corrects himself.

Heartache washes through me. I shake my head and glance to the window. The sky is clear outside, yet it doesn't feel like the sun is reaching into the room.

"Danny," Ryker says as he leans forward.

I shake my head again, trying my best to regain control over my emotions. It's a simple slip-up, but still, it hurts like hell because it will probably be true. Ryker might have a daughter one day… just not with me.

And I want that for him. I want him to find happiness after me.

Still, it will mean I'm dead.

He'll meet a new woman, and she'll be the one he loves. The one he makes love to.

"I didn't mean it that way," he murmurs.

I close my eyes when the deep ache spreads through me. I can fight this all I want, but at some point, my time will run out.

RYKER

Dammit, I fucked up.

Badly.

I move onto the side of the bed, and framing Danny's face, I try to get her to look at me, but she won't. She sucks in a quivering breath, and it breaks my heart that I just hurt her.

Leaning closer, I press my forehead to hers. "I'm sorry."

"But it's true," she whispers brokenly. "One day, you'll have children. Just not with me."

Pulling slightly back, I shake my head, and then she finally opens her eyes. "I won't. Unless it's with you, there's no way I'll have children."

The fear returns to Danny's face. "We both know the surgery was just a temporary fix. No matter how hard I fight, the day will come when I'll die of this."

I shake my head harder. "I refuse to believe that. The radiation and chemo will take care of whatever's left."

"My chances of having kids as well," she whimpers.

Fuck.

I straighten up, then I shake my head again. "There has to be something we can do."

Danny weakly lifts a shoulder. "Like?"

Right then, Sarah comes in. My gaze snaps to her. "Isn't there a way we can preserve Danny's eggs?"

"Oh yeah. Hasn't Dr. Friedman spoken to you about preserving your eggs?" Sarah asks. Both Danny and I shake our heads, and it has Sarah saying. "Let me page him."

My lips curve slightly as I turn my eyes back to Danny. "See, there is something we can do. Okay?" I lean over her and press a tender kiss to her mouth. "I fucked up, but at least it led to this conversation so we can plan for the future."

Danny gives me a weak smile. "Yeah."

We have to wait an hour before Dr. Friedman comes to see us. After we explain everything, he says, "It's something we offer all our patients when they're facing radiation and chemo. We can extract your eggs and keep them frozen until you're ready to have children."

"But will I be able to carry a child?" Danny asks, her voice tight with tension.

"Yes. The radiation and chemo only affect your fertility, not your womb," Dr. Friedman explains.

Danny lets out a relieved sigh. "When can we do the procedure?"

"I'll have it scheduled with an OB/Gyn for the day before you start with radiation." Dr. Friedman gives Danny a warm smile. "Any other questions." When she shakes her head, he moves closer. "Let me check everything while I'm here."

I stand back and cross my arms over my chest as I watch Dr. Friedman do his checks. Once he's done, I smile and murmur, "Thank you."

"I'll see you tomorrow."

When he leaves the room, I move back to Danny's side. Her eyes meet mine, and I'm relieved to see the fear has retreated. Still, I ask, "Feeling better?"

She nods.

I sit down again and take her left hand in both of mine. "Have you ever thought of baby names?"

Danny shakes her head. "Not really."

I pull my phone out and search baby names, and then I hold the screen so Danny can see. Starting with boys, I murmur, "Peter. Definitely not Noah."

It draws a smile from Danny. "I like Elijah."

My eyes dart to hers. "Yeah?"

She begins to get into it. "Or Ryder. Like a combination of our names. Kind of."

Smiling, I nod. "Well, that sorts out the name if we have a boy."

When Danny chuckles, I let out a breath of relief, then I say, "Now for girls. We've got Olivia, Ava, Isabella, Amelia, Harper…"

Danny pulls a face. "I don't like any of those. Do you?"

Shaking my head, I search for more names. "How about Ella, Grace, Leah?"

She shakes her head again, and then she thinks for a moment. "Ryelle? Does that sound weird?"

"It's unique," I murmur, then test the name, "Ryelle." Tightening my hold on Danny's hand, I smile. "A little bit of me and a little bit of you."

Danny lowers her gaze before looking at me again. "I really want to have a child."

"As soon as you're better, we'll make it happen," I grin.

Danny's smile grows a little more, and then we just stare at each other until her eyes drift shut.

Chapter 26

DANNY

The past week has been busy. Yesterday my eggs were harvested, so at least there's that.

I'm scheduled for an MRI and then my first radiation session. Dr. Friedman said I should be able to go home afterward.

I'm nervous, but I'll just have to get used to it. I'll be receiving radiation Monday through Friday for the next six weeks. At least I get weekends off.

"What are you thinking about?" Ryker asks.

"Radiation. Going home," I murmur. My gaze lifts to his. "You should go back to work. I can get a chauffeur to bring me for the treatments.

"That's not open for discussion," Ryker disagrees. "I'll bring you."

"Yeah, but work –"

He shakes his head. "Work's not going anywhere. My dad's filling in for me. Stop worrying about Indie Ink. Just focus on yourself. Okay?"

Tilting my head, I ask, "What are you going to do at home all day?"

His lips instantly curve up. "Look after you... love you."

"I'll probably sleep most of the time," I mutter.

"Then I'll just stare at you," he jokes. Ryker takes a deep breath. "There's a couple of things I want to do around the house. I have plenty to keep myself busy with."

"You're not going to change your mind, are you?" I ask. When he shakes his head, I lift my hand and brush my fingers over his jaw. "I need to apologize in advance."

"For?" he asks.

"Any throwing up and hair shedding I might do." I try to play it off as a joke, but in reality, it's embarrassing.

Ryker immediately picks up on it, and locking his eyes on mine, he says, "Don't worry about that, Danny. I've read up about the side-effects. I know what to expect." He turns his face, pressing a kiss to my palm. "You getting better is all that matters."

I brush my thumb over his stubble. "You're perfect."
He begins to shake his head, and it has me giving him a stern look. "You're perfect, Ryker."

Sarah and the oncology nurse come into the room with a wheelchair. "Time for the MRI and radiation."

"Can I come along?" Ryker asks.

"Of course." Sarah grins at us. "I think it's amazing how close the two of you are. Couple goals."

Her comment fills me with warmth. "It's all Ryker. He's the best."

He helps me out of bed and into the wheelchair, then he presses a kiss to the top of my head. "When you get the woman of your dreams, it's easy."

As we leave the room, Sarah asks, "Have you always loved each other, or was it something new that crept up on you?"

"I've always loved her," Ryker replies.

Sarah glances at me, and it has me saying, "Honestly, I felt like a perv for crushing on him when he was a senior." My comment has Sarah frowning, so I explain, "I'm almost seven years older than Ryker."

She glances between us. "That can't be. You look the same age."

"What age is that?" I ask.

"I'd guess around twenty-seven, twenty-eight."

"I'm totally taking that as a compliment," I chuckle. "Ryker's twenty-five, and I've just turned thirty-two."

She lifts an eyebrow at me, then looks at the oncology nurse. "She doesn't look thirty-two, right?"

"Hell no. Not like any thirty-two-year-old I've ever seen. I had a truckload of wrinkles by then."

Ryker leans down and whispers in my ear. "See, the age gap doesn't bother anyone."

I let out a silent burst of laughter, then admit, "Fine, you were right."

Entering the room, Ryker makes the nurses swoon when he picks me up then sets me down on the bed for the MRI. "Careful, Mr. West," I murmur. "You'll have all the nurses crushing on you."

"Too late," Sarah laughs as she pushes the wheelchair out of the room.

Ryker just shakes his head, a sexy smile playing around his lips. "I'll be on the other side waiting." He gives me a tender kiss then leaves so they can start the scan.

While I lie still, I send up a prayer it will show the growth is gone. As soon as the scan is complete, Ryker comes back into the room. His expression is filled with love as he slides his arms beneath me, and then he gives me a kiss.

Wrapping my arms around his neck, I say, "A girl can get used to being carried around."

He lets out a chuckle then places me back in the wheelchair.

I'm taken to another room, and this time the oncology doctor is present. I lie down on the bed, and once everything is ready, my stomach churns with nerves.

I hear clicking and buzzing noises, and after a short while, fatigue sets in. By the time the fifteen minutes are up, I'm nauseous and struggling to stay awake.

This time I have zero energy to joke with Ryker. We make it back to my room in the nick of time, and then everything I ate comes up.

Sarah helps me while Ryker keeps rubbing my back and where I thought I'd be embarrassed, I couldn't care less now. I feel too sick to worry about what anyone thinks.

RYKER

God, this is hard.

Danny finally stops vomiting, but she's completely drained. It has me asking, "Does this mean she's staying?"

Sarah shakes her head. "No, she should be good to go home. Obviously, we have to wait for Dr. Friedman to check on her one last time."

Nodding, I ask, "Can I place her back in bed?"

"Sure."

I slip my arms under Danny, and her head just falls against my chest. It has me murmuring, "I've got you, sweetheart." Once I have her back in bed, I rush to the bathroom to wet a cloth. Using some bottled water, I help Danny rinse her mouth, and then I wipe over her face and neck.

Within seconds she's asleep, and then I drop down on the chair beside the bed.

"How did it go?" Aunt Della asks as she and Uncle Carter come into the room.

"As well as can be expected," I whisper, not wanting to wake Danny. "She just fell asleep."

Uncle Carter comes to stand next to me, and placing his hand on my shoulder, he gives me a squeeze.

"Would you like to sit?" I ask.

He shakes his head. "I'm good."

We all stare at Danny for a moment, then I whisper, "She vomited."

Uncle Carter squeezes my shoulder again. "Thank you for sticking with her through this."

"There's nowhere else I'd rather be."

For the first time in a long while, Aunt Della meets my eyes, and then she smiles. "We're lucky to have you."

Her words mean a lot to me, especially after taking their power to make medical decisions about Danny away.

Dr. Friedman comes while Danny's still asleep, but he touches her shoulder. "Danny."

She begins to wake up, and he gives her a moment for the grogginess to fade, then he says, "Your MRI looks good." He holds it up so we can all see, and my eyes lock on the black spot where the tumor used to be.

God, that thing left a hole in her head.

Dr. Friedman looks happy, though. "I'll prescribe you something for nausea. Okay?"

Danny nods. "Please."

"Great. I'll leave the prescription with your paperwork. I'll see you next week."

"Thank you for everything," Uncle Carter says.

We shake the doctor's hand, and then he leaves. "I'll take our bags to the car, then I'll come back for you," I say as I begin to gather all our belongings.

Aunt Della comes to help me, and when she picks up the photos, I say, "Can I take those with us? Just so Danny has them at home."

A smile spreads over Aunt Della's face. "Of course."

When I have everything, I take it to the car and pull the vehicle closer to the entrance. I jog back into the hospital and sign Danny's discharge papers. After getting the prescription, I stop at the hospital's pharmacy to get the meds. Walking into Danny's room, she's sitting up on the side of the bed, talking to Sarah.

"I'll see you tomorrow," Sarah says, giving Danny a hug.

"Thanks for everything," I say as we help Danny into a wheelchair.

"You're welcome."

Sarah pushes the wheelchair as we leave the room. Reaching the exit, Danny begins to stand up, and it has me darting forward. When I lift her to my chest, she whispers, "You don't have to carry me everywhere."

"I'm not letting you walk right after you've had radiation," I mutter.

Uncle Carter opens the passenger door for me, and once I place Danny down on the seat, I turn to them. "You're coming home with us, right?"

The corner of Uncle Carter's mouth lifts. "Of course."

I walk around to the driver's side and slip behind the steering wheel. Reaching over Danny, I pull on her seat belt, then I grin at her. "Finally, I get to take you home."

Resting her head against the headrest, her lips curve up. "Home."

"Our home," I murmur as I start the engine.

Danny drifts off during the drive, and when I pull up the house, she's still out cold. Climbing out of the car, I go open the front door before going back for Danny.

Uncle Carter parks behind me, and when I lift a sleeping Danny out of the vehicle, Aunt Della says, "My poor baby. She must be exhausted."

They follow me into the house and to the bedroom. Aunt Della pulls the covers back so I can place Danny on the bed.

I watch as Aunt Della covers Danny, then I say, "Let me bring in the bags, then I'll get us something to drink."

"Just point me toward the kitchen, and I'll make us all some coffee."

Uncle Carter sits down on the bed and knowing he's staying with Danny, I show Aunt Della the kitchen and where everything is.

After everything is taken care of, we carry extra chairs up to the bedroom, and then we all watch Danny while she sleeps.

Chapter 27

DANNY

It's been two weeks since I started radiation, and I feel like shit warmed over.

I don't vomit as much anymore, but I'm always nauseous. I'm still taking it as a win. Even though I'm tired all the time, the fatigue usually lifts within an hour of receiving radiation. The part that really sucks? I'm starting to lose my eyebrows and lashes. Soon I'll look like a fish.

Pulling a disgruntled face, I leave the bedroom. As I'm coming down the stairs, I hear Ryker in the kitchen. Walking inside, the corner of my mouth lifts when I see he's busy cutting chicken breasts into strips.

"What are you making?"

His head snaps up, then he grins. "Chicken and cobb salad."

He's been taking care of all the meals, refusing to order in. I take a seat at the kitchen table, then say, "Let me help."

Ryker shakes his head. "You just relax. I've got this."

Leaning my elbows on the table, I stare at Ryker.

Before we started dating, I knew Ryker was a catch. I mean, I fell in love with him after all.

But this man standing in front of me... there really aren't any words to describe how phenomenal he is.

Ryker glances up again, and seeing that I'm staring at him, he asks, "What?"

Lightly, I shake my head. "I'm just admiring the man in front of me."

His mouth curves up into the sexy smirk I love so much. "Yeah?"

"Yeah. Take your time preparing the salad. I still have a lot of admiring to do."

He lets out a silent chuckle.

My eyes drift over his strong jawline, and tilting my head, I murmur, "If it weren't for your strength, I don't think I would've made it this far."

Ryker's hands still, and then he lifts his eyes to mine. "Don't underestimate yourself."

Shaking my head, emotion pushes up my throat. "When I fell in love with you, I thought it was because you were so damn handsome. Turns out that wasn't the case. It was the strength I saw in you. Most men would run for the hills when they find out the woman they've been dating for five weeks has cancer. But not you."

"Most men are idiots," he mutters.

"Also true," I chuckle. "Still, you're incredible, Ryker."

He adds the chicken to the salad, and after plating our food, he washes his hands. "You know what, I'm totally taking the compliment," he tries to joke it away. Turning back to me, he asks, "Where do you want to eat?"

"Out on the patio." I get up and grab two bottles of water from the fridge.

Ryker brings our food, and he waits for me to sit down before he hands me my plate. "Looks yummy," I murmur, even though I don't have much of an appetite these days. My weight has dropped, so I eat whatever Ryker prepares. I can't stomach anything heavy or spicy, which means I've been living on salads, soups, and fruit.

While we're eating, I mention, "I'm thinking of returning to work when I start with chemo."

Ryker stills, and he takes a deep breath before he replies, "Let's wait and see how you feel after your first chemo treatment."

Tilting my head, I ask, "Are you always this protective, or is it just because I'm sick?" Then I remember how he was in Cape Town and the weeks after we got home. "The answer is always, right?"

He lets out a chuckle. "Pretty much." He spears a strip of chicken then glances at me. "Does it bother you?"

I shake my head. "Not at all."

"Good," he murmurs.

It begins to rain, and we watch the drops falling from the sky while we finish eating. When we take our plates back inside, I place them in the dishwasher. As I straighten up, Ryker's arms wrap around me from behind. Turning around in his hold, I rest my arms on his biceps, and then I look up.

Seeing the love Ryker feels for me written in his eyes makes my abdomen tighten, but it fades quickly when I remember what I look like.

"Thanks for lunch," I whisper as I push up on my toes. I press a quick kiss to his mouth, and when I try to pull away, he tightens his hold on me.

When I lower my eyes to his neck, Ryker asks, "Why do you do that?"

I glance up quickly before looking away. "What?"

"You've been getting uncomfortable when I touch you."

My gaze flies back to his. "I don't." Ryker tilts his head, and it has me admitting, "I look like a damn fish." A frown instantly forms on his forehead. "I don't feel attractive," I mutter.

Ryker moves a hand up to the side of my neck. "Do you want to know what I see when I look at you?"

I nod.

The corner of his mouth lifts. "One hell of a bad-ass woman. God, Danny. You're beating cancer. Give yourself some credit."

"I know," I mumble. "But I still look like a fish."

Ryker takes hold of my hand and pushes it down between us until my palm rubs over his erection. My eyes snap up to his.

"Do I need to make it any clearer that you're still as beautiful as you were two months ago?"

I shake my head, and when Ryker lowers his head, I begin to slowly rub my palm over his bulge. Desire trickles through my veins as his mouth hovers over mine. "How do you feel?"

"Like a woman who needs her man to fuck her," I murmur, and it has him crashing his mouth to mine.

His hands frame my jaw as his tongue thrusts into my mouth, stroking hard against mine.

I work to unfasten his belt, and when I finally have his hard length free, I begin to stroke it as my desperation for him spirals out of control.

Ryker makes quick work of my sweatpants, and then he lifts me onto the kitchen table. The kiss is filled with hunger as he pushes inside me with one hard thrust. I let out a satisfied moan against his lips, my hands moving up his back until my fingers weave through his thick hair.

I've missed him.

So much.

Ryker breaks the kiss and, pressing his forehead to mine, our eyes lock as he begins to thrust harder. His hands grab hold of my hips to keep me in place, and seeing the naked hunger on his face makes my orgasm build at the speed of light.

Moans begin to drift over my lips, and it makes his features tighten until he looks primal.

I slump back on the table, and then my body tightens as a powerful orgasm rips through me, stealing my ability to breathe.

When Ryker begins to jerk inside me, a hot as hell grunt escapes him, and it only increases my pleasure.

His thrusts turn short and hard, and all I can do is moan from the residual pleasure pulsing through me.

When he stills, Ryker places his hands on the table on either side of my head and stares down at me.

"I fucking love you, Danny." He begins to pull out but then drives back into me. "I love your body. I love your soul. I love everything that makes you who you are."

I begin to nod as tears blur my eyes because here I am, looking my absolute worst, and Ryker still wants me.

If that's not true love, then I don't know what is.

RYKER

Danny's handling chemo much better than she did the radiation. The last MRI came back positive, with still no sign of the tumor returning.

Slowly she's starting to plan things again, and I don't think she even notices it.

I'm cleaning the grill for the barbeque we're hosting to celebrate Independence day. Everyone's coming over to our place, bringing something to eat.

Danny comes out of the house, and then I do a double-take and just stare at her.

Holy fuck, she looks gorgeous.

"What do you think? Is it stupid?" she asks, probably referring to the wig.

"I think you look breathtakingly beautiful," I answer, but then add, "As long as you're comfortable, babe."

"Does it look fake?"

I shake my head. "Not at all. It looks like your own hair did."

A wide smile spreads over her face. "Thank God. It took me a while to find the right one."

When our friends and family start to arrive, everyone points out how good Danny looks, and it has her basking in the compliments.

She needed this to build up her self-confidence after the knock it took.

"Princess," I hear Uncle Rhett holler, and glancing into the house, I watch as he swoops her up into a hug. "Damn, look at you all healthy and pretty."

"Thanks, Uncle Ledge," she murmurs, and then they just hold each other.

People are starting to forget that Danny has Glioblastoma. They probably think Danny's beat it, and that's the end of that.

Not me. It's always in the back of my mind that it can come back at any moment. It forces me to live in the now, to appreciate every second I get with Danny.

The only way I keep from losing my mind to fear is by telling myself Danny still has a lot of fight left in her. Honestly, I could die in an accident next week. No one really knows when their time's up, and living in fear of the end just ruins the entire journey.

Hunter and Jade head my way, and wiping my hand on a rag, I reach out to shake his before giving Jade a hug. "Hey, guys, thanks for coming."

"Wouldn't miss it for the world," Hunter grins.

"Where can I place the potato salad?"

I gesture to a table. "Over there."

By the time everyone's here, there's a permanent buzz of conversation in the air, and every couple of seconds, I hear a burst of laughter.

There are three distinct groups. The older generation is seated under the canopy, and all the girls are sitting with Danny on the other side of the veranda.

The guys are standing with me while I grill steaks.

Seeing Danny smile makes my lips curve up. She needed this.

"When are you getting married?" Jase asks.

I glance back at Danny. "Once she's done with the chemo, we'll set a date."

"She looks great for someone who's going through chemo," Noah states.

"She's a fighter," I grin. "I don't think there's anything she can't do or beat."

Hunter shakes his head at me. "Wow, you're madly in love with her."

I let out a chuckle. "I never said I wasn't."

"Hold up," Tristan suddenly says. "So, all the time you wanted to spend at my house was actually because of Danny?"

I begin to laugh, and when he lunges at me, I dart out of his reach. "Only partly," I quickly reply, but it doesn't stop Tristan from coming after me.

He locks his arms around me, and then we're both falling into the pool. When my head breaks through the water's surface, I hear everyone laughing.

Danny's cracking up, her arm wrapped around her waist, and the sight sends a burst of warmth through me.

After Tristan and I climb out of the pool, I'm glad to see Hunter's taken over, grilling the steaks.

We head up to the bedroom, and I chuck a pair of cargo pants and a shirt at Tristan. He catches it with a grin, and once we're both dressed in dry clothes, he says, "I have to admit, I had my doubts about you and Danny dating."

"But?" I raise an eyebrow at him.

"You make her happy, and..." Tristan lifts his hand to my shoulder. "There's no one else I'd rather have for a brother-in-law. Thank you for loving her the way she deserves to be loved."

We give each other a brotherly hug. "It means a lot to me to hear you say that," I murmur as we leave the room.

When we step out onto the veranda, I hear Dash say, "We're having twins."

I begin to chuckle. "Double the diapers."

Dash rubs a hand over her pregnant belly. "I'll have Miss Sebastian helping me, so I'm ready."

Danny leans forward, glancing between Fallon and Dash. "Aren't your due dates close?"

"Yeah, we're a week apart," Fallon answers. "December babies."

Tristan goes to stand behind Hana, then he says, "Ours is due March."

"What?" The word explodes from me.

"You're having a baby?" Aunt Della suddenly says, popping into the conversation.

Tristan lets out a chuckle. "Yeah. Hana's already four weeks pregnant."

My eyes turn to Danny to see how she's handling the news, but there's a happy smile around her lips as she shares in her family's joy.

As soon as she's recovered from all the treatments, we need to start working on our family.

Chapter 28

RYKER

My fingers tighten around Danny's as Dr. Friedman holds up the MRI scan.

She completed the chemo a month ago. Honestly, I don't think there will ever come a time where my heart will not beat out of my chest while we wait for the results of an MRI.

Dr. Friedman smiles, then says, "Still clear. The progress you've made is promising, Danny. I'm happy." He tilts his head as he looks at her. "How do you feel?"

"Relieved. Better. My hair's starting to grow back." She pulls a face. "It's more fluff than hair, but still, it's something."

"Don't worry about your hair. Eventually, it will grow back," he tries to encourage her.

"How long do we have to wait before we can start planning for a baby?" I ask.

Danny's head snaps to me, then back to Dr. Friedman, who answers, "I'd say a year. Just to be on the safe side."

"That gives us time to get married," I chuckle.

Again, Danny glances at me, her mouth curving up.

"I'm expecting an invite to the wedding," Dr. Friedman jokes.

"Oh, definitely," I assure him. He gets up from his chair, and it has us rising to our feet. "I'll see you in three months."

"Thank you for everything," I murmur as I shake his hand.

Danny goes to give him a hug, and I hear her whisper. "Thank you for the time you've given me."

"You're welcome."

When we leave Dr. Friedman's office, I wrap my arm around Danny's shoulders and pulling her tightly to my side, I press a kiss to her temple, murmuring, "Another win."

She grins up at me. "Another win."

As we walk to where the car is parked, I ask. "How do you feel about celebrating in Cape Town?"

I've been planning the trip so we can celebrate her being cancer-free. Christopher and her parents are in on it, seeing as they'll have to fill in at Indie Ink for her.

Danny frowns as she climbs into the passenger side, but she waits until I slide in behind the steering wheel, then she asks, "When?"

"The flight is scheduled for Thursday night."

Her mouth drops open. "Seriously? That's two days from now! What about work?"

"I've spoken with your father and Christopher, and they have it all handled."

Her eyes widen. "Oh my God, you're serious. This isn't a joke?"

I shake my head. "As serious as can be."

Danny thinks for a moment, then she surprises me by nodding instead of arguing with me. "Okay, let's do this."

"Really? You're okay with it?" I ask to make sure.

"Yes." A wide smile spreads over her face. "Let's go back to Cape Town."

"Great. Your dad said he'll come in tomorrow to take over whatever you're busy with at work."

"Get me back to the office. There's a lot I need to take care of."

Letting out a chuckle, I mutter, "I get a feeling we're not going home tonight."

"That's for sure."

The corner of my mouth lifts. "Still a slave driver."

"Hey, I'm not that bad. I've been going home at six every night since I returned to work."

"True."

"And since Jade started working, it's helped take the load off me," she adds.

"Things are coming together nicely," I murmur. Noah completed his Law degree, which is helping with my workload, as well.

Sitting on the plane, we've just flown over Niger when Danny snuggles against my shoulder.

I let out a soft chuckle as I maneuver my arms underneath her, and getting up, I lift her to my chest.

"This feels familiar," she mumbles sleepily.

"Sleep, babe," I whisper as I carry her to the bed. My grin widens as I put her down, and when I lie down facing her, my smile widens when she snuggles up against my chest.

To think, nine months ago, I thought that moment would be all I'd ever get. Now? Now she's mine.

Wrapping my arm around her, I press my mouth to her hair that's starting to grow into a buzz cut, and I take a deep breath of her.

Damn, she still smells good.

Where I used to live for the moments I got to flirt with her, I now exist for every second I get with her. I love her more than ever, and with every passing day, that love just keeps growing. She's woven into every part of my life. She's everywhere I look. Danny's my life.

Slowly, I tighten my arm around her, keeping my mouth pressed to her head.

Loving Danny… it feels like it's my sole purpose for existing.

I'm the man who gets to make love to her.

I'm the man who comforts her.

I'm going to be the man who gets to change her last name.

I'll be the father of her children.

God. God. God. Thank you.

Thank you for not taking her from me.

Moving my hand up until I reach her neck, I soak in the feel of her soft skin. Danny presses closer to me, then she murmurs, "My gravity. That's what you are. Without you, I'd just be floating around in empty space."

I move my hand to her jaw, and tilting her head back, our eyes lock. "Good, because without you, I'm nothing."

I claim her mouth, and when my tongue brushes over hers, my eyes drift shut from how good she tastes.

We savor every second of the kiss, never taking anything for granted.

DANNY

Ryker got us a room at the guesthouse, where we made love for the first time. Out in the countryside, the air is fresh, and it looks like it's going to be a nice day.

We're following a path through the orchards, listening to the birds chirping. It's one of the things I love most about South Africa. It's never quiet.

His fingers tighten around mine, and glancing up, I take in the handsome man at my side.

That's where he's been since our first trip to Africa, right by my side. Ryker never wavered. To think I was worried about a relationship between us not working out.

The thought hits me that when Ryker said he loved me the first time, he knew exactly what he was saying.

My lips curve up, and it has him asking, "What are you thinking about?"

"The first time we had sex," I admit.

"Yeah? What about it?" he asks.

"You said you remembered all of it. Right?" When Ryker nods, I ask, "So even though you were drunk it was something you wanted?"

"Of course." I stop walking, and Ryker turns to face me. "It wasn't just a drunken one-night stand."

I let out a chuckle. "Damn, there goes the only one-night stand I ever had."

His smile grows, then he asks, "I know we're not supposed to ask these things, but how many were there before me?"

My eyebrows pop up, then I tease him, "Seeing as it's too late for you to leave me, I'll answer."

A frown instantly forms on his face. "How many, Danny?"

I shake my head, wanting him to call me by my first name, and I get my wish when he tilts his head, muttering, "How many, Daniele?"

I let out a burst of laughter. "Three."

His frown deepens. "Excluding me?"

When I nod, he shakes his head. "Three men I have to kill. Tristan will help."

I begin to laugh harder, and tugging at his hand, we start to walk again. "And you?"

"You're gonna laugh," he mumbles, and it has me pulling him to a stop again. Then he mutters, "One, and as you know, she traumatized the shit out of me."

I give him a wide-eyed look. "Are you serious?"

Ryker nods, his gaze locking on mine. "I wasn't lying when I said I've only loved you. I tried to date that one time, and after a month, I called it off because it felt like I was cheating on you."

Emotion washes over my face as I stare at Ryker. "Just when I thought I couldn't love you more…"

His mouth curves up into the sexy smirk I love so much, and then he lifts my left hand to his lips. "Let's get married, Danny. Not a year from now. As soon as possible."

Pulling my hand free from his, I lift it to his jaw. Standing on my toes, I press a tender kiss to his mouth, then I murmur, "I'm sure I can plan a wedding in a couple of weeks."

"So, two weeks from when we return to the states?" Ryker asks, his eyes darkening with excitement.

"The first week of December," I agree, and it has Ryker yanking me to him and claiming my mouth with a hungry kiss.

Then it hits me. I'll get to spend Christmas with Ryker and my family. I'll be here to see Christopher and Tristan's children being born.

I'm even thinking less of the fact that I have cancer.

Had.

You had cancer, Danny.

You beat it.

You were sick, and now you're better.

That's how I'm choosing to look at it.

If it comes back, I'll beat it again… and again because there's no way I can let go of Ryker.

I'm determined to have a future with him, to have his children.

My lips curve against his, and then I whisper, "In a month, I'll be Danny West."

"Say that again," he murmurs.

"Danny West."

Ryker kisses me with the intensity of all his love… the very love that kept me from dying.

Epilogue

DANNY

Three years later...

I've been feeling sick the past week, and it's getting harder to hide it from Ryker.

I can't sleep. I can't eat.

Fear claws its way up my spine as I park my car outside the hospital.

I know Dr. Friedman warned me that most cancer patients don't survive past five years, but I was hoping I'd be one of the few to make it.

When the headaches and nausea returned, my stomach bottomed out. Part of me wants to put my car in gear and get out of here, not wanting to know whether the tumor has returned. The other half of me knows that's not an option. Not if I want to get ahead of this thing.

Just to think that I'll have to go through the surgery, radiation, and chemo again makes my heart shrivel.

But I'll face it all again if it means I can get another three years with my husband.

My phone begins to ring, and seeing it's Ryker, I quickly answer. "Hey."

"Where are you?"

My heart begins to beat heavily in my chest. Ryker will be so angry if he finds out I'm hiding this from him.

Shit, I should've told him.

Closing my eyes, I admit, "I'm sitting in the parking area at Cedars-Sinai."

"What?"

"I'm at the hospital. I'm seeing Dr. Friedman in twenty minutes."

"Wait for me. I'm on my way."

Before I can get another word out, Ryker cuts the call.

Emotion pushes up my throat as I climb out of the car, and after shutting the door behind me, I lean back against it. I try to focus on my breaths.

It's going to be okay.

Shh…

It's going to be okay.

Minutes later, I see Ryker's car as he pulls into the parking area. When he gets out of the vehicle, he jogs toward me.

"I'm sorry," I begin to ramble. "I should've told you when the headaches returned. I was just... scared."

Ryker's features are tight with worry as he nears me, and then his arms wrap around me. "I'm here." He pulls back, his eyes locking on mine. "When did the headaches start?"

"A week ago. I've also been nauseous," I spill the beans.

"Fuck." Ryker keeps an arm around me as he glances at the hospital. "Let's go, or we'll be late for the appointment."

My legs feel like lead as we walk toward the entrance, and with every step, my body tightens and my heart shrivels. Panic begins to build in my chest, and I come to a sudden stop, shaking my head. "I thought I could, but I can't." I take a step backward. "I can't do this again."

Ryker pulls me closer to the wall, and then his arms lock around me. "You can, Danny. You can."

Tilting my head back, I whimper, "What if this is it? What do we do then?"

"This isn't it," he growls. "I told you I'm never letting you go, so you'll just have to give it your all again. For me. For us."

317

I begin to nod, but Ryker still has to pull me to Dr. Friedman's office.

We're shown to an examination room, and the moment I walk inside, my heart pounds against my ribs. "Oh God," I whisper as my breaths rush over my lips.

Ryker lifts his hands, and framing my face, he stares deep into my eyes. "Deep breaths, babe. I've got you."

Dr. Friedman comes into the room, a warm smile on his face, but the moment he sees our worried expressions, it fades. "This can't be good."

"Danny's having headaches again, and she's nauseous."

"Okay, let's do some tests before we start worrying. It can be anything. It doesn't mean the tumor has returned."

Ryker pushes me down on a chair, and Dr. Friedman orders a nurse to draw blood while he begins with the usual checks, then he says, "Even though it's unlikely, let's do a pregnancy test as well."

"Really?" I ask.

"There's always the possibility."

I follow the nurse to a restroom and pee in a cup. When I walk back into the examination room, I hear Ryker ask, "If the tumor is back, what are our options?"

"Same as before," he says, "I'll remove what I can, and then we start treatment."

"How many times can you do that before it's not an option anymore?" Ryker asks as he pulls me down to sit on the chair next to him. His hand clasps mine tightly.

"It all depends on Danny's health and how far the tumor has spread."

"Hopefully, we caught it in time," Ryker mutters.

Minutes later, the nurse comes back in and hands Dr. Friedman the pregnancy test.

When his mouth curves up, my eyes widen. "What? Am I pregnant?"

He lets out a chuckle. "You have something growing inside you, and my guess is it's not a tumor."

"Danny's pregnant?" Ryker asks, his hand almost crushing mine.

"Yes. Looks like the two of you are all about performing miracles."

"Oh my God," I whisper as surprise washes over me. Then the relief hits, and I let out a sob. "Oh my God."

"I'll refer you to an OB/Gyn so we can work closely together, seeing as you'll still have to go for your quarterly MRI scan."

Ryker and I sit frozen, just staring at Dr. Friedman, and it draws a burst of laughter from him. "You're having a baby, Danny."

Another sob burst over my lips, and then Ryker yanks me to him.

"I'll leave you to bask in the happy moment. Stay as long as you want." I hear Dr. Friedman leave, and then I cry from the intense relief and happiness overwhelming me.

Ryker pulls back, and then he kisses me even though I'm a blubbering mess. When his eyes meet mine, and I see the happiness shining from his eyes, it's impossible not to ugly cry.

"We're having a baby," he whispers with awe.

I begin to nod. "A little Ryder or Ryelle."

"You know what this means, right?" he asks. When I shake my head, he says, "You're going to be a mom, Danny."

My chin quivers as I nod. "The mother of your child. Our little miracle."

RYKER

Ryelle – 6 Years Old.

There are regular kids, then there's Ryelle.

She's bouncing in the backseat as we pull up to her school. The moment she sees all her uncles, she lets out a high-pitch scream.

I pull a face as I glance at Danny, who looks like she's about to cry.

"We're here! Let me out!" Ryelle yells. I get out, and the moment I open the door, she's out of the car like a lightning bolt and running toward her grandfathers.

My father-in-law catches her, and she gives him a wet kiss before she reaches for my dad. All the men crouch down, so they're eye level with her.

She presses wet kisses to their cheeks as she mumbles, "Love you, Uncle Ledge. Love you, Uncle Jax. Love you, Uncle Marcus." Then she moves onto the younger generation. "Love you, Uncle Christopher. Love you, Uncle Tristan. Love you, Uncle Noah." Ryelle stops to catch her breath, and placing her hands on her hips, she mutters, "Phew, this is hard work." Then she continues, "Love you, Uncle Kao. Love you, Uncle Jase. Love you, Uncle Hunter. Love you, Uncle Forest."

When she's finally done, she glances back at Danny and me. "Can I go in now?"

Danny lets out a sputter, and it has me saying, "What about Mommy?"

"Ugh. Do I have to? I'll see you after school," she sasses me.

"Just like her mother," I mutter to Danny, then I crouch, "It doesn't matter, Ryelle. Come give us a hug."

Ryelle pushes out her bottom lip. "Fine, but make it quick."

When her tiny arms wrap around my neck, I stand back up and hold her tightly to me. "Love you, princess."

"Not half as much as I love you," she whispers.

I pass her over to Danny, and when she hugs our daughter, emotion pushes up my throat.

Every day is still a miracle for us.

"Love you, my princess," Danny murmurs. "To the moon and back."

"Love you, Mommy," Ryelle whispers. "Further than the moon and back."

I let out a chuckle, and then Ryelle squirms out of Danny's hold, and the moment her feet touch the ground, she runs for the entrance.

Taking hold of Danny's hand, we follow after our daughter, who's way more prepared for her first day of school than we are.

DANNY

Ryelle – 18 Years Old.

My eyes are glued to Ryelle, where she's standing with the other kids.

She's starting at Trinity Academy.

God, where has the time gone? My baby's an adult.

It's a pity my nieces and nephews graduated last year. I would've felt a hell of a lot better if they were here to look out for Ryelle. At least she's not alone. Forest and Aria's son is starting his final year. There's also Fallon and Kao's youngest son, who's the same age as Ryelle. And next year, Jade and Hunter's daughter will start at Trinity.

Again... where the hell did all the time go? It feels like just yesterday, I found out I was pregnant with Ryelle.

"What are you thinking about?" Ryker asks as he wraps his arm around my shoulders.

"How quickly time has passed. It's hard to believe Ryelle is starting college."

"Yeah, you know what that means, right?" I shake my head, and it has him chuckling, "We're getting old."

"Yeah, I can see the gray coming through," I tease him. Pressing a kiss to his mouth, I murmur, "You're the hottest father here."

Ryker gives me that sexy smile I love so much. "With Ryelle at college, we'll have the house to ourselves."

"Yeah, we do," I grin at him.

"It's me, you, and the kitchen table the second we get home," he grumbles.

I let out a chuckle as I turn my gaze back to Ryelle, and then I watch as Liam, Forest and Aria's son, wraps his arm around my daughter's shoulders. I begin to slap Ryker's abs. "Look."

The instant Ryker sees what I see, his body tenses, and then I'm dragged toward the group of kids. "Ryelle, let's go grab your bags so you can move into the suite."

Liam quickly lets go of her, and it earns us a scowl from our daughter. She frowns at her father. "It can wait."

"Hell no, it can't," he grumbles as he grabs hold of her hand, and then Ryelle's tugged away from Liam.

Feeling sorry for Liam, I say, "Want to help us?"

"Sure. Yeah. That would be great, Mrs. West."

He falls into step next to me, and I can't stop myself from laughing when I watch Ryker and Ryelle frown at each other.

"Lord, I pity anyone who tries to date Ryelle."

"Why?" Liam asks, his eyes snapping to mine.

I point at Ryker. "You'll need to get past her father first." Patting his shoulder, I add, "And then there are her uncles, her grandfathers…" I give him an encouraging smile. "You should survive, though. I'm a firm believer in miracles."

The End.

Those of you who have followed this series from Heartless, keep reading for a letter from Miss Sebastian.

Dear Bedazzled Reader

My angel-girls. (And chunk-of-hunks if there are any)
I can't believe the time has come to say goodbye. This
crazy author whose books you keep reading refuses to give
me my own story, so I'm sneaking my bedazzled ass in
here because come hell or high water, I will have my say.

I've felt your love for me through every page.
Oh Gawd. One sentence and my eyes start leaking.
Deep breaths.

I hope you all find your own happiness in life. At times
things might get hard, but you have to lift your chin and
say, "Not today, Satan. Not today. My bedazzled ass will
make it through this."

Life is short. Grab it by the sparklies and make it your
biatch.
Learn to love yourself the way I love myself.
Don't apologize for who you are, the same way I owned
who I am.
I love all your bedazzled asses. So much. Without you, I
never would've existed.
Okay… my make-up is totally ruined now.

I love you all. Every single one of you.
Don't let anyone steal your sparkle. You keep shining.

xxx
Miss Sebastian.

Want to read where it all started?

Go 1 Click HEARTLESS.

And when you're done with the Enemies To Lovers Series,

follow it up with Trinity Academy.

All the sale links are listed in the back matter of the book.

Want to read where it all started?

Go 1 Click HEARTLESS.

And when you're done with the Enemies To Lovers Series,

follow it up with Trinity Academy.

All the sale links are listed in the back matter of the book.

The Heirs

Reading order of future releases:

Coldhearted Heir
Novel #1
Hunter Chargill (*Mason and Kingsley's son*)
&
Jade Daniels (*Rhett & Evie's daughter*)

Arrogant Heir
Novel #2
Jase Reyes – (*Julian & Jamie's son*)
&
Mila West – (*Logan & Mia's Daughter*)

Defiant Heir
Novel #3
Kao Reed (*Marcus and Willow's son*)
&
Fallon Reyes (*Falcon & Layla's daughter*)

Loyal Heir
Novel #4
Forest Reyes (*Falcon & Layla's son*)
&
Aria Chargill (*Mason & Kingsley's daughter*)

Callous Heir
Novel #5
Noah West (*Jaxson & Leigh's son*)
&
Carla Reyes (*Julian & Jamie's daughter*)

Sinful Heir
Novel #6
Tristan Hayes (*Carter & Della's son*)
&
Hana Cutler (*Lake & Lee's daughter*)

Tempted Heir
Novel #7
Christopher Hayes (*Carter & Della's son*)
&
Dash West (*Jaxson & Leigh's daughter*)

Forbidden Heir
Novel #8
Ryker West (*Logan & Mia's son*)
&
Danny Hayes (*Carter & Della's daughter*)

Stand Alone High School Romance

Black Mountain Academy Series

Not My Hero
Colton Lawson
(Brady from Coldhearted Heir's Brother.)
&
Brie Weinstock
(daughter of Serena from Trinity Academy)

Trinity Academy

FALCON
Novel #1
Falcon Reyes & Layla Shepard

MASON
Novel #2
Mason Chargill & Kingsley Hunt

LAKE
Novel #3
Lake Cutler & Lee-ann Park

JULIAN
Novel #4
A Stand Alone Novel
Julian Reyes (*Falcon's Brother*)
&
Jamie Truman (*Della's Sister – Heartless, TETLS*)

THE EPILOGUE
A Trinity Academy Novella

Enemies To Lovers

Heartless
Novel #1
Carter Hayes & Della Truman

Reckless
Novel #2
Logan West & Mia Daniels

Careless
Novel #3
Jaxson West & Leigh Baxter

Ruthless
Novel #4
Marcus Reed & Willow Brooks

Shameless
Novel #5
Rhett Daniels & Evie Cole

False Perceptions
Novel #6
A Stand Alone Novel
Hayden Cole *(Evie's Dad)*

Saint Monarch's Academy

Coming 2021

St. Monarch's Academy.
The only neutral territory where the heirs of the
wealthiest crime families are forced to rub shoulders.
You're either a predator, a pawn, or the prey.
Alliances are made.
Loyalty is owned.
Love is taken.

These books will all be
STANDALONE/Suspense Romance

MERCILESS SAINTS
End of April

CRUEL SAINTS
End of May

RUTHLESS SAINTS
End of June

TEARS OF SALVATION
October
Alexei Koslov's book
A spin-off for The Underworld Kings Collaboration

Connect with me

Newsletter

FaceBook

Amazon

GoodReads

BookBub

Instagram

Twitter

Website

About the author

Michelle Heard is a Wall Street Journal, and USA Today Bestselling Author who loves creating stories her readers can get lost in. She resides in South Africa with her son where she's always planning her next book to write, and trip to take.

Want to be up to date with what's happening in Michelle's world? Sign up to receive the latest news on her alpha hero releases → NEWSLETTER

If you enjoyed this book or any book, please consider leaving a review. It's appreciated by authors.

Acknowledgments

Wow. Here we are. I can't believe this journey's come to an end but thank you to each and every reader who has loved these characters as much as I do.

To my alpha and beta readers, Taylor, Donita, Sherrie, Sheena, Allyson. Kelly, Elaine, Sarah, and Leeann – Thank you for being the godparents of my paper-baby.

Candi Kane PR - Thank you for being patient with me and my bad habit of missing deadlines.

Sybil – Thank you for giving my paper-babies the perfect look.

To my street team, thank you for promoting my babies.

A special thank you to every blogger who has stuck it out with me to review this entire series. I know it was hard, but I'm so grateful for you.

Love ya all tons ;)

Made in United States
Troutdale, OR
11/18/2024